PRAISE FOR

TRANSMISSION

AT THE HEART OF *TRANSMISSION* I FOUND A STUNNING DRIFT—a wide and generous current able to hold contradiction and paradox, and somehow, time itself. Here is a drift to surrender into; one punctuated with despair and radical love, one that might reveal a new story of what home and recognition can mean. J. E. Sumerau offers a voice that is really a plurality of lyric intensities; it reminds me of a river, if a river could bloom.

—SELAH SATERSTROM, AUTHOR OF
Rancher, Ideal Suggestions, & Slab

J. E. SUMERAU IS ONE OF MY FAVORITE AUTHORS AND *TRANSMISSION* **DOES NOT DISAPPOINT.** Once again, Sumerau leaves her unmistakable fingerprint on this beautiful story. Reading this sensitively and compassionately written novel, you will become swept up in Millie's journey, which although unique, is also sure to resonate deeply with any reader. The ending is inspiring and pure perfection. Highly recommended.

—PATRICIA LEAVY, AUTHOR OF
Celestial Bodies: The Tess Lee and Jack Miller Novels

J. E. SUMERAU'S LATEST NOVEL, *TRANSMISSION* OFFERS A CAN'T-MISS KALEIDOSCOPE OF BEAUTIFUL, RAW, AND EXPLORATORY REFLECTIONS narrated by Millie Morrison, a protagonist making sense of how her past intersects with her present. Just as captivating as the story are Sumerau's characters, a diverse group of queer and poly individuals. Written in a stream of consciousness, Sumerau's work invites not only Millie to contemplate and process past loves, trauma, and relationships as she carves out her future in the next phase of her life; this format invites the reader to do the same, to sit with our difficulties and nostalgia alike, and to determine what's holding *us* back from carving out our life's path. *Transmission's* authenticity asks us, through Millie, to not only reflect on how we can improve our relationships with others, but perhaps most importantly, our relationship with ourselves. We root for Millie to achieve catharsis through the novel's myriad transmission of narratives—from her childhood to adulthood. And on a personal level, perhaps we can do the same for ourselves, too. *Transmission* is a perfect fit for personal reading, as well as those in sociology and gender & sexuality studies.

—SHALEN LOWELL, AUTHOR OF
Gender Optics

WINNER OF
THE GEORGE GARRETT FICTION PRIZE

*Established in 1998, The George Garrett Fiction Prize
highlights one book a year for excellence
in a short story collection or novel.*

SELECTED BY
SELAH SATERSTROM

—AUTHOR OF *Rancher, Ideal Suggestions, & Slab*

TRANSMISSION

J. E. SUMERAU

★trp
the university press of shsu
huntsville, texas
texasreviewpress.org

Library of Congress Cataloging-in-Publication Data
Names: Sumerau, J. E., author.
Title: Transmission : a novel / J. E. Sumerau.
Description: First edition. | Huntsville : TRP: The University
  Press of SHSU, [2023]
Identifiers: LCCN 2022048666 (print) | LCCN 2022048667
  (ebook) | ISBN 9781680033168 (paperback) |
  ISBN 9781680033175 (ebook)
Subjects: LCSH: Self-acceptance--Fiction. | Self-actualization
  (Psychology)--Fiction. | Conduct of life--Fiction. |
  Travel--Physiological aspects--Fiction. | Oviedo (Fla.)--
  Fiction. | United States--Description and travel--Fiction.
LCGFT: Epistolary fiction. | Psychological fiction. | Domestic
  fiction.
Classification: LCC PS3619.U457 T73 2023 (print) | LCC
  PS3619.U457 | (ebook) | DDC 813/.6--dc23/eng/20221019
LC record available at https://lccn.loc.gov/2022048666
LC ebook record available at https://lccn.loc.gov/2022048667

FIRST EDITION
Cover & Inset Woodcut: "Where the Fallout Blows"
by Stefanie Dykes
Book design by PJ Carlisle
Printed and bound in the United States of America
TRP: The University Press of SHSU
Huntsville, Texas 77341
texasreviewpress.org

FOR XAN,
THANK YOU EVERY DAY FOR EVERYTHING.

Okay—*I get that*—I do kind of act like a child. I'm *okay* with that.

I wonder what you're doing today. I thought about asking you this morning, but, *I don't know*, you seemed kind of, *I don't know, different*—or maybe just annoyed or tired or something like that. You seem that way a lot since we got back here. You just come and go without a word. I don't *know* why. I know you won't like this, but it reminds me of those two years, *you know?*—right after we got out of Florida, when you weren't around, and I was all by myself all the time—I didn't like that (it wasn't *right*—we're a team, *remember?*); I'm not saying you mean to be, well, distant, but *that's* what it feels like.

Maybe *that's* what you were talking about last night at the probably-even-more-demolished-this-morning ballpark. Maybe you're going through something. Maybe I'm going through something. *Maybe* it's just the latest shift in whatever we are to each other. I know when I worry you always say I should "write it down." That's what I'm doing. I'm transcribing myself onto the page, opening the wound, whatever you want to call it. But it doesn't seem to help. (I know, *I know*, I hear you in my head—*I get that;* sometimes it takes a while.)

"Write it down," you'd say, "and keep doing it until you feel better," you'd say, and that's what I'll do, *okay?* I will, but—not to make light of your comments (I don't want to start a fight or anything, I really don't)—but it feels *different* this time. It just feels, *I don't know*, it just feels like this is a whole, new *something*, you *know?*—like you used to say every time we moved on to the next city or the next home, "it feels like a shift is happening," and I guess I have to "make sense of it, my way" as you always say, but it feels strange to me.

Shit, the Karen-look-alike is heading this way; I guess she just needed a refill.

I was hoping she just gave up—but she's looking at me.

WONDER IF YOU'VE BEEN OUT TO OVIEDO. Have you? I haven't made it that far yet, I admit. I *know* that was the reason I wanted to move back here for a while, I wanted to see where we came from, but I haven't worked up the nerve yet.

Of course, I could have handled my grandmother's land the same way other people do, through the mail, through a broker, but I thought it would be a good chance to take stock of things. It just sits there, of course, and I could have just stayed somewhere closer to it while we're here (it hasn't sold yet, and no one else is staying there)—I just don't feel like I would want to be in Oviedo long enough to need to get some sleep. I like sleeping at the place we have in Winter Park. I *know* it's temporary (that's kind of the point, *right?*) but I like it. There's just enough space (not too much, not too little, just enough) and that encourages me not to add anything I don't need. You always said I needed encouragement. I never disagreed.

I don't *know* why I came here today. I could get equally good soup at many other places. There is, after all, a *Jason's Deli* only a few miles from this spot, and yet, here I sit. Maybe it's because we spent so many nights in that bookstore in Tampa right after we left here (do you *remember* those nights?)—we would get cheesecake (always two different types, so we could each have more than one flavor), and we would eat and laugh and read books we couldn't afford to buy. The cheesecake probably wasn't the best choice for dinner so many nights in a row, if any, but it was tasty, "it felt like being rich," you said, and it was just a short walk from the room we rented in Carrollwood at the time. Were we even inside the city limits of Tampa at that point? (Do you *remember* the peacocks we found on that back road?—wow, it still baffles me—we *couldn't* have been in the city, *right?*—not a chance I would say, but I don't *know*.) I *do* know we moved down to the south part of the city *after* I got that job waiting tables, thanks to the guy who thought I had a cute ass (was his name Derrick? Darren? I'm not sure). He had wavy hair and a shell necklace (which you thought was odd.) We were in the city *after* that, I *know*, but was the place in Carrollwood *in* the city?—I'm not sure. I guess I could look it up, but sometimes I just prefer to wonder.

Maybe *that's* it. *Maybe* this whole thing is about nostalgia. I was trying to think about the last time we were in Florida; even *that* was a while ago. It seems like yesterday. But first, there was Tampa . . . *that's* it: it was the summer of 1998, a few months after "the-things-we-don't-talk-about," but before "the-couple-years-we-spent-apart," and we'd headed west on I-4 because you said you "needed the gulf." I guess I was following you—the way I followed you into year after year of more baseball even though it was torture for me—the way you followed me here this time. You *needed* the gulf then for some reason, and I wasn't ready to say goodbye to you (if I *ever* could be) so we went west together like hippies in a van, but only a few miles really. We stood on the sand at the gulf a couple of times over the next six months: the two months of Carrollwood seemed to flash by, and the four months in the south part of the city, in that dilapidated bedroom of the even worse-off house on Gray Street (oh, how I hated that place) seemed more like a dream than anything. I still don't know what type of dream, sometimes it's like a nightmare when I think about it, but sometimes it seems sweet, like something out of a coming-of-age movie. I'm not sure which of these versions to trust, but maybe *this* is the answer—*maybe* it's like Roy at the auto parts shop in Gainesville told us in 1999: "Don't trust anything too much and you'll do alright in this world, *I tell ya what.*"

Why do I *remember* that? *Maybe* because *that's* what a lot of life feels like? Maybe not. Of course, we met Roy because of the lady with the broom *(remember her?)* She just showed up at our dirty-ass room in south Tampa. She was screaming mad at someone *(us* maybe? I don't *know)* and she started throwing your CDs. It was like a siren, that sound, her screams: *Danger, Danger,* a warning transmission, alerts dancing along the airwaves. I never knew what to make of it. I dreamed about the sound for years. I could not place it or forget it, no matter how hard I tried. Then one day, it was just gone (well, I guess it wasn't gone since I can *remember* it now—but it didn't bother me the way it once did, I guess *that's* what I mean), it wasn't so painful, somehow; time must have done that.

We hit the road—*remember?*—it was the only answer we ever had. Something goes wrong, anything, no matter what: hit the road as fast as you can (*somewhere*, we thought, *it must be better.*) Of course, all these years later I realize that we were dreaming about *that* too.

I got a job moving parts for that auto shop and Roy let us live in his garage. Everyone was curious about Y2K. We stayed there for about four months until we heard about the chance to go to community college in Tallahassee, and maybe use *that* to get a *real* college degree. It was another pipe dream, another wish along the next interstate. Never happened, of course, but the idea was a pretty one. We sat in that garage talking about real college campuses like we knew anything about them. We thought it would be like the movies. We *thought* that, but we didn't *know* anything at all. We thought we would just show up and figure it out (how did we know so little, I often wonder)? We grew up down the road from a university. We had a campus right there. We never visited. We never looked around. We didn't even check out the brochures or anything. It was just scenery. It was like something we thought we understood—only to realize it was nothing like what we had imagined.

Maybe *that's* why I wanted to get a cup of chili at the *Barnes & Noble* on Colonial tonight, maybe *that's* it. The *Barnes & Noble*, like the little bookstore at the beginning of our travels, might have been the only thing that was like anything we expected to find along the way. Cuddled together in those semi-padded chairs, all our short years brimming with optimism and dreams; we didn't *know* we didn't know. We would find out later, but for those moments, for just a second, we could believe it would all make sense one day. Maybe *that's* why I wanted subpar soup; I wanted something to remind me of the days when everything still seemed at least kind of possible, when it really felt like there was something *different* in the next town.

I WAS THINKING ABOUT NEW ORLEANS the other day. I'm not sure why. I was just sitting at the *Drunken Monkey* enjoying a peanut butter brownie, you know the vegan ones we like, and wondering whether or not I felt like looking at records. I wasn't doing anything special. I wasn't even thinking about going out drinking or anything like that. I was just letting my mind wander in between chapters of a Stephen King novel, and I kept turning the dial in my head back. It must have been around 2008, yeah *that*'s right, because I remember Obama was running for office for the first time and he was elected that year.

I was thinking about the night Marty got so trashed at that piano bar in the French Quarter. We were staying in those rooms over off Carondelet—*remember* that place?—it was near the *Holiday Inn Express* that later became some kind of boutique hotel—*remember?*—it had those comfy arm chairs and the window that seemed too big? I remember you stood by the window laughing. Your silhouette was smiling at me—you were standing there laughing; that much I'm sure of. You said you were thinking the window might collapse, and wouldn't it be odd to just fall out and never know why. I didn't think it was funny. You did. We didn't argue, but we could have.

I remember Marty and I made what some people call "love" in one of those chairs a few days later, I think it was the beige one (I wanted the purple one, but I was never all that assertive)—Marty was *more* than assertive enough for everyone. I was too sore to think about it much the next couple days, but he was so much fun in small bursts. Anyhow, I was thinking about the night we went out to the piano bar.

11

I remember Marty got *so* drunk (he kept saying he wasn't, but we *knew* he was) and Carla was joking that she would play the piano by the end of the night to show them how it was done. We were drinking hurricanes, well, *they* were. You were drinking something you got from the guy with the eye patch, and I wasn't in a drinking mood. At some point, I *remember* Sebastian showed up, but he seemed funny or off, like he was on something—maybe he was. I was watching Marty. He was cute when he wiggled his fingers, remembering his childhood piano lessons with the nun. He was so drunk he was sure there was a secret club somewhere—*remember?*—he knew exactly where it was.

He dragged us—me, you, Sebastian, and Carla I think it was—he dragged us all through the streets, past that goofy little face-painting stand, past the art gallery that always says the art is not for sale, past the place that has something to do with sisters going to court, past that late-night market that was more like a boutique—or maybe was just *weird* looking—with so much wine you had to wonder if there were any grapes left in the world at all. We went roaming through the streets. Marty kept almost falling and saying the place was just around this or maybe that corner, and you thought it was stupid, but it was also kind of fun—*I* thought so at least.

I remember you thought I could love Marty—*do you remember that?* I thought I *did* love Marty, but you said I wasn't there yet. Marty thought I couldn't love anyone. I *remember* he told me that—another night after too much drinking—at a bar that did not have pianos; he said I was broken.

I asked you about it. You said he didn't understand. I told you *I* didn't understand. You said I would *someday*. I still don't. I *remember* we finally got to the place, the secret place of course, and found it was so secret it didn't exist—*remember that?* You went away to look at something, but I don't remember what you said you found. Anyway, Marty was *sure* it was there. So, there we were—Marty in his scarf and checkered shirt and Carla with her lipstick smeared in an awkward manner—Sebastian was humming "Everybody Hurts," and it was kind of funny, I remember, because he had just broken his hand the weekend before and he had this ugly kind of orange-meets-hell-colored cast.

Anyhow, Marty was *so* sure it was there he started pounding on the window (he was *crazy*) it was this display window at the front of a store. He was yelling, but I couldn't tell at *what* or *who*, well, not at first. He was just *wild*. Then Carla started yelling too, and Sebastian asked if anyone had any smokes and no one answered, but we all had smokes and so did Sebastian, and then I realized that Marty was yelling at the dress on the mannequin or maybe the mannequin itself or *maybe* both, and I just started laughing and I don't *know* why it was so funny but Sebastian lit a smoke and I took it, I don't *know* why I took it, and you weren't around for a few minutes, but you *were* later, and then Marty was peeing on the window like a *lunatic* and all I remember after *that* is we went to Krystal's.

DON'T WANT YOU TO WORRY ABOUT ME.
I *know* you do. And I *know* I've been more emotional since we came back here, and especially in the last few days. And that *last* message last night sounded like I was drinking but I really wasn't, I promise, it's *okay*, I'm doing fine, just getting the feel of being so close to home again, I guess; *I don't really know*—but I'm *okay*. Are *you* okay? Don't worry, though, *I'm okay* and *we're good*—I can feel it even now. It's not about you, *okay?* I promise. It is not even about the "miss you" stuff that happened out by the likely-now-all-the-way-gone park the other night; I'll figure that out and just keep writing until I do, *okay?*—no problem. That's not a big deal, and it's not even about that, not even a little bit. Don't do that *thing* where you think you know better than me; it is not about any of *that*.

Believe it or not, it's about Peter.

I keep thinking about him every time I pass *Peter's Kitchen* on Colonial.

You *know* how I love hot dogs at times (for some odd reason you can't figure out)? Well, I drive out to the *Hot Dog Heaven* sometimes, *you know?*—on East Colonial?— that's as far east as I've made it (I know, I *know*) for some reason I keep forgetting that I can get from that area we like on Corrine to Colonial further down, and I keep going down Bumby by mistake, so I drive past *Peter's Kitchen* on the way. Each time (I don't *know* why) it makes me think about Peter. I *know* how you hate for me to repeat things, but you know how important it is for me to *think* about things so I'm going to do it. You can skip ahead, (I *know* you will) it's *okay*, but I need to think through this:

Peter Berry was born the same year we were (the year 1980) and in the same little town of Oviedo, just on the east side of Orlando. Okay, *that's* simple enough. He had the same kind of childhood *we* had, *you know?* he really did. He lived in a neighborhood that I've read is being kind of *changed* right now, but he was always around at the park. I think he played soccer, like the other kids who were terrible at baseball and basketball—"Who knows why anyone would play such a boring game," you used to say.

But maybe it was something else.

I always thought he was our friend, but I don't *know* if he was. I think sometimes that happens when people teach you important things about life. I think sometimes they become more to you than they really were, but you don't see it at the time. I think that happens. I don't *know* why. I'm sure *you* have some damn theory about it. (You seem to have some theory about every damn thing, but that's *okay*, its fine, I love you for your weird theories and ideas about all kinds of shit.) So, I remember that Peter was born later in the year. He was only seven when the accident happened, and we were already eight.

We would be listening to R.E.M. on the radio like cool

kids, though I don't *know* if that seems so cool all these years later. We would be sitting at the park; you would be playing with one of your cassette booklets (how many places did you leave those pages over the years?—if I ever kept count, I lost it. "Sometimes," you said, "I feel like I need to leave my mark on the world;" I *remember* those words *so* well, it sounds *so* cute to me now, but I always wondered about it back then). Anyway, you were tearing out one of the pages of your booklets and thinking of something to draw, I'm sure, and I was probably sitting there on the sidewalk or one of the posts in front of this-or-that plaything, cracking jokes or something—I was *so* talkative back then—*so* strange to think of it now, that we would just be *sitting* there like we did. And Peter would come walking or rolling by with his skateboard. He always stopped for a couple seconds, and I would say something because I knew you would not, and he always seemed *so* scared and lonely and shy and awkward, especially when we didn't speak to him right away. Like one day, I asked about his "wheel things," and he said something about skateboard "trucks" I didn't catch, and I said something about mom's mechanic boyfriend and he laughed, but it didn't seem that funny to me. It was like that. It was always like that—is *that* friendship?—I don't *know*. Maybe it *was* at that age. Or maybe he just felt like *something more* because of the accident later.

I mean, it wasn't like it was unusual that he was riding a four-wheeler, at seven. Kids, seven and eight, did that all the time. The one he was riding just hit a rough spot and flipped, "simple as that," as your mom said, "it could have happened to anyone," *that* was the phrase, *that's* what caught our attention I think: "it could have happened to anyone." That was it. We didn't know much yet, but we knew *we* were anyone. It was "a warning, a lesson, a life lesson," as ol' George (who sat on the steps of the old firehouse) would say over and over again through his drool when we walked past there to the other park, later.

It could happen to anyone, I remember thinking. I *remember* thinking about that, hearing those words in my dreams for *so* long after that. I guess it should have prepared us for some of the things we would see later, but I'm not sure it did. I think *that's* why I wonder about the depth of our connection: Was it a friendship?—or was it just that Peter transmitted something so important to us that I *had* to see him as a friend later? Was it friendship?—or just the fact that we couldn't stop thinking about him, about *him* being *anyone*, about *us* maybe even being *him*? Was *that* it? Were we *ever* friends with Peter?—or did Peter become a symbol we started thinking of as a close friend later to make sense of the accident? the lesson? the *fear*, I guess, would be the most honest way to put it.

I don't *know*, but these kinds of thoughts are why I might seem more emotional now because I can't stop asking these questions (now that I'm *so* close to where we grew up), even if I *can't* get all the way over there to the far-east side of the city just yet.

DID YOU KNOW THEY HAVE TAPES in the record stores again? Do you remember when we used to find tapes everywhere, and make our own? I was *thinking* about this as I stood in the record and tape store (*Retro*, I think it's called) over by the 408 expressway or whatever it's called. I was looking through the racks, racks, and racks of tapes (believe it or not) and staring at a couple we had when we were kids. It was such an amazing experience, just to see them there, and somehow more emotional than I would have imagined (I actually teared up a little bit, to tell you the truth). I was standing there holding a copy of *Document* (remember that special R.E.M. tape we all *had* to have back then?) and I found myself shaking just a bit (not *too* much) and I felt my shoulders kind of heave and flex in that way they do when the tears are coming. As I sometimes do (as you *always* do), I thought about getting out of there, but it was a good feeling overall, I don't *know* why, but it was nice, so I just stood there holding the old, beat-up, used-by-however-many-people-and-for-however-many-years cassette tapes in my hand—and felt tears softly swim down the lines that age has given my face.

It was like that night in the studio apartment with Alex—*remember I told you?*—when Alex touched me on my thigh in that sweeping motion, twirling their tiny fingers in what felt like a *semi*-semi-circle, as our bodies were joined in that special (sometimes not so special—but special-*always*-with-Alex) way, on the futon with the never-quite-able-to-get-it-clean-enough sheets, and I felt myself shake somewhere deep inside I didn't know existed yet, and I shuddered (both in the usual, and in a *new* way) as I felt tears start dropping against my cheeks—*do you remember that? Do you remember what you said?*

You said it was like "walking between dreams and realities, between rooftops and bottom floors, between invitations and parties, somewhere in space where the real and imaginary become fluid ideas—almost magical," you said, "and for just a few moments we can see, feel, experience, and even *transmit* the interplay of the universe between us."

I don't *know* if that was *really* it (what you said). I don't know if *any* words could capture it *really*, but I remember I liked the way you put it. It felt *right*, if that makes any sense at all, it felt *right*.

Anyway, I was thinking about this moment, and for some reason my mind went on a little vacation to those weeks we spent in 2012 Charlotte. It was "a magical detour," as Margo put it, when she picked us up on her way back to the place we were all sharing in Wilmington later in the week, the one owned by the older lesbian lady in Southern Pines who we met by chance in that abandoned cemetery. We went riding on the train in Charlotte, *remember?*—we just had to see what the rest of the area looked like, and we were so tired of walking downtown even though that diner (you remember the one that looked like something out of *Beverly Hills, 90210*?) was amazing. We went riding on the train, and then you saw that *El Salvadorian Café* (I still don't know how you spotted it, your eyes must have had some superpowers or something) and we got off the train. I remember there were families in the café, *do you remember?* There was just a little boundary (kind of a curtain) in between the two sides of the dining area, and we sat there in that plastic booth-type thing, laughing and eating food and laughing some more like we were kids again. You were saying something about basketball when the lady in the not-quite-as-plastic-looking booth across the room mentioned picking up records next door.

I remember we both wondered how we didn't see the record store. We were shocked, but then we went outside, and realized the years in New York and Chicago and Atlanta had shifted what we thought of as "next door" at some point without us noticing the change. It was in the shopping center "next door." We walked and kind of skipped over there hand-in-hand like we had all the time in the world because, well, it always feels like we *do* when we're together. We skipped right over that pole that somehow fell, *and remember?*—you made up stories about how it landed in the middle of a parking lot without anyone seeming to give a damn. We laughed when the little kid asked if I was a boy or a girl, and you said you wondered if people would always "want to know," or if "that religion will die at some point like so many others." I felt like I needed a bottle of water, but the gas station guy looked scary so you said I should just pretend to only speak Spanish (so he would be annoyed like he was with the customer in line ahead of us) and get me out of there fast. I did it. He was annoyed. You thought it was hilarious. We got to the record-store-that-we-hoped-would-look-like-the-ones-from-our-childhood; it was just a storefront that could have been a *Dollar Tree* or any other boring place. There were no big signs, no hipster culture was in sight, and no bars nearby. It said "tapes" in the window, and you said, "yeah *right*," and we went through the whole place, *remember?*—we looked everywhere but there were no tapes, just vinyl and CDs, *remember?*—and there was this utterly perfect-looking person (that was also somehow such a massive personality with a tiny body), smiling, while trying to hold a stack of what seemed like 30-or-so CDs in their arms, and you thought it was *so* cute (we both did) and even more so when their companion, *whoever they were*, offered to help or get a basket, and they were adamant that *these* were *their* CDs, and the two hugged in the middle of the store.

And just like them (back in 2012 with their CDs) I was holding my tapes in *Retro*, (R.E.M and Springsteen's *The River*) and smiling about those days back in Charlotte, when I started thinking about the way we used to dig through the bins (always budget bins back then, of course) in those New York shops in the even-earlier early 2000s (*remember* when you found that *Pink Floyd* record that is now worth so much—for three dollars?) and we would get any tape or vinyl we wanted for less than a pack of cigarettes because the world seemed to have forgotten that they could be loved, so they sat alone, looking almost scared (or maybe just sad) in the budget bins, packed together like children awaiting the train from the orphanage in some Charles Dickens novel, or something waiting for us to give them a hug and play with them, or *play them* in the secondhand stereos we somehow managed to fill that apartment with (off of Houston Street) back then. (*Do you remember* the one with the broken latch that always turned every cassette into a Chipmunks' cover of whatever song was playing? I *loved* putting in Megadeath or Pat Benatar or even that surprising little Death Cab for Cutie tape we found, and listening to Alvin, Simon, and Theodore show us how those artists would sound at a different pitch). Did I ever tell you that sometimes I think about those tapes and records in those bins? (I don't *know* if I did, *maybe* I did.) They spoke to me in some way I've never figured out. There was *something* about them (lonely, abandoned, unwanted, with no place they could belong, as far as they knew) that always made me think of how I felt when we were growing up, and even on our travels across the country. They just *sat* there (I felt in my dorkiest and sappiest moments) waiting and wishing for *someone* to want to hold them, to hear them—to pull them from that place they didn't fit—into some better tomorrow.

I don't *know* why I just thought about all that. I know it's not *really* about what we talked about that night in the park behind the record store; it's not the *same*, but it felt right for some reason—*I don't know*. You're probably laughing at me as you listen to this, or maybe that's just my own insecurity talking—*I don't know*. I guess I just wanted to share what it felt like to hold those tapes in that shop (it is *so* strange that I could have them *all* for less than an eighteen pack of beer. I wonder what *that* says about our country's opinions of the arts, of history, of the things that *were* and what they *become* when they are no longer the best or *only* option available)—but it seems like *too* much (after already tearing up) just standing there holding a few old cassette tapes.

YOU STARTLED ME A LITTLE BIT when you showed up this morning; I don't *know* why. I guess I should just be used to you coming and going as you please, but sometimes it still surprises me that you haven't left for good yet.

I don't *know* how you put up with me, honestly, but I'm so glad you do. Remember when we were kids?—what were we, like nine or something?—and you kept saying I was your "favorite insect" because you actually wanted me to keep bugging you? It was a cute thing, a kid thing, to say, I know, *so* simple, but I still carry it for some reason. It's like that old set of ever-evolving cassette booklets you kept in your backpack pocket, where you said the things you might need at any moment should live, back then. You would whip one out at the most seemingly random times and just draw a picture on it and leave it behind for someone else to find. I spent years wondering how people reacted if, or even *when* I guess, they found the damn things, but I never came up with a very good answer, which, as you kept saying, was, of course, "the whole point of leaving pieces of yourself wherever you wanted to" in the first place. You said it was about *"appearance* and *disappearance* mixed together in a fragile, heartfelt moment of clarity where you became both whole and empty." I always wished I could put things into words in the ways you do.

You were cold this morning, but not in an emotional way, you just kept shivering. I offered you a blanket, but you didn't want it. You said you "felt *something,* like, fading away."

I didn't understand. I often don't understand.

You said it wasn't important because "it was natural." You always say "nature is supreme whether or not we want it to be." It would drive you crazy the way people would try to explain this-or-that thing about nature without nature being able to talk back, as if people somehow knew the facts because other people would believe them. You would go on these rants and I would listen for—what was it? seconds? minutes? hours? days?—I'm not sure, time didn't make much sense. You said that was a sign of love. I didn't understand that either, but you said neither did you. You kept rubbing your arms and hugging yourself the way you did when we were so much smaller, the way you did to feel *okay* when you didn't know how to feel *okay.*

I was worried. You said I shouldn't worry so much. We agreed to disagree. We often do that, don't we?

You were quieter than usual this morning. You didn't say much; it was more like talking to myself.

I wondered about that after you left. I didn't say anything; you would have told me I worry too much. That's *okay,* cutie. I know I worry about *everything,* and in so many ways, you have so often felt like *everything.* Alex says that's the way it is supposed to be when you find real love. I don't *know* if they're right. Margo used to ask questions about you and get annoyed that I would never answer. I guess it just helped to keep you all to myself back then, and I don't know *why* or *how* that changed.

You said you liked that I was writing. You said it sipping your coffee. You were drinking out of the same mug that Brianna gave you for your sixteenth birthday. I can't believe you kept that thing for over two decades. I guess we all have things we just cannot let go. Or maybe we don't really choose what we let go of and what we don't. Maybe it's more complicated than that.

Maybe some things touch us too deeply to ever really go away.

You said you would be out and about for a while. You said you were staying somewhere else to gain a different perspective. You said you wouldn't be around tomorrow morning.

I wanted to protest or at least ask some questions. I wanted to say something important (something we know I'm not all that good at) but I *know* you need your time. I *know* your time to yourself (wherever you go, whatever you do, whoever you meet) feeds you and *us* in some way I don't quite understand. It's like that time we were at the *Galleria* in Houston after eating cheesecake and macaroni balls, and you just *needed* (you said it was *that* deep, a *need* you couldn't control or explain), you just *needed* to watch the ice skaters. We stood in the mall watching them for two hours that day. I didn't understand it, and I probably never will. Maybe *that's* the case with your departures over the years (or maybe not, *I don't know*).

I can feel your hand on my back. I can *feel* it, but I know you're not really here—not now.

THE OTHER DAY I FOUND A PLACE I wish would have existed when we were kids. I finally made it over to Oviedo, though, don't ask, I didn't make it into our old neighborhood yet. I will.

"I was just driving down this road" (to use your own words about the night we found those dancers in New Orleans all those years ago), and I stopped to make sense of what seemed like a random carnival that had sprouted up out of nowhere. It wasn't in Oviedo, I should say, I was on my way back, after chickening out before I even made it far enough on Central to get some pancakes at *The Townhouse*, if you can believe it. It was on the other side of the now-huge college campus, so maybe I was already back in Orlando, but hard to tell. I did that thing where I took a wrong turn and *found* something.

You always said it was funny how much of life that habit of mine captured.

As usual, *I don't know why*, but I pulled into this parking lot to check out the sights and sounds of the carnival (I know, I *know*), I didn't want to go to the carnival, but I wanted to *be* with it, if that makes any sense. I kept moving across this nondescript shopping center toward the flashing red-and-white lights of the Ferris wheel; I could hear you saying "Bueller, Bueller," like you always did when I said "Ferris wheel" when we were kids, and I stopped because there was this tiny coffeehouse nestled in the corner of the shopping center; *The Coffee Factory*, I think that's what it was called, but I don't remember for sure because all I could think was that it reminded me *so* much of that *Sertino's* place in Texas that it was hard to breathe. I just *had* to go in, and for a moment even the beautiful, green-and-yellow fluid flashing of the lights on the ride with the elephants disappeared from my mind, despite how much I've always loved those colors, and anything that, as you put it, "even comes close to being elephant-related."

So, I went into this coffeeshop and it was even like *Sertino's* on the *inside*: it had the same kind of plastic buckets in the lobby that you *know* came from *Target*, but you pretend are more special, full of beans and one of those signs to tell you where the LINE STARTS even though any idiot could theoretically figure it out. You *hated* those signs. I thought your hatred was adorable. The place was smaller than the *Sertino's* we found in Port Arthur, but about the same size as the one in Beaumont (the one near that stand where I just kept having to go back for breakfast tacos every damn day the whole six months we called that little piece of East Texas home. Do you remember the name of that taco stand? I don't, but I kind of want to know now. Maybe I should visit there next after I get up the courage to see our old neighborhood, but maybe not). Anyway, I was using that idiotic (though no more or less idiotic than usual, I admit) structure called "the restroom"— two single occupancy places gendered for no apparent reason other than maybe to announce they are practitioners of that particular religion—when I started laughing too hard and had to sit on the floor for a second as "It's the End of the World as We Know It (and I Feel Fine)" started blaring through the speakers. I just lost it for a minute laughing at the thought of us dancing to this song as kids only a few miles down the road from a coffee place beside a carnival.

You will be proud of me. You *know* what I'm talking about, and you *know* I did it. You also know I did it just for you: I waited. You will be, however, disappointed in the source of the music because they violated the new rule you invented in 2004 that day we stood outside the tire place wondering how we were going to afford the new (what did Mary call them?) car shoes or something, that Mary desperately needed. Nope, sorry babe, I love you, but they did not share your belief that "It's the End of the World as We Know It (and I Feel Fine)" should always, without exception, no matter the reason, be followed by "Bad Day." I waited just in case they did what you so deeply love for some reason, but they did not. The next song was some janglepop-type thing from, I'm sure, one of the bubblegum factories that gave us the beauty of New Kids on the Block and the horror of every terrible pop band. I admit I considered giving a public service announcement about this, the same way Michael did for us in that coffee shop, *Murky*, I think it was called, in D.C. that one time, but again I just kind of chickened out like I had on the way to our old neighborhood.

I think I like this coffee place though. I mean, I spent like an hour outside watching the carnival lights and I bet I'll go back. They have cheesecake, the plain kind I like so much, and it's the kind where they don't serve it completely cold or too warm from whatever source so it's both kind of gooey and still solid. I enjoyed the slice I had with a cup of coffee that likely came from one of the bins of beans at some point. As I sat there, though, I kept thinking about the time we spent in Port Arthur or as you always said, close enough to call it Beaumont so we don't sound like small town folks. I'll never forget Lem, *remember her?* with the strawberry blonde hair and the obsession with finding the perfect dildo from each sex shop in Texas, almost falling out of her chair matching your shocked expression when that girl in the Port Arthur Starbucks gushed over how excited she was to shop in Port Arthur because it was so amazing to be *in the city*. Now, I must admit, I wonder if Lem ever completed her mission.

I feel like we had more fun in the Beaumont, Port Arthur area than we should have been able to, but I'm not sure why. I think, in the end, it was like so many things—it was about being together, goofing around, and feeling free for a little while. I think that was it. I sometimes wonder if *that i*s the meaning of life all the churches and scientists seem so obsessed with, *you know*, the people in our lives and the times we spend with them. Lem would say I'm talking about "intimacy," but I'm not sure if I still even understand what that is. Of course, *maybe* that's the point. Maybe some things are too powerful or "fluid" (or some word I don't *know* yet) to ever truly be understood. At the same time, I think back to our nights in *Sertino's* laughing about this or that stupid television show we watched, thanks to the free cable in Lem's apartment where we stayed every night. I think about the hours we spent sitting outside on that little concrete patch beyond the glass doors while Lem was inside doing whatever. I *remember* how we could hear her often singing along to this or that old pop song.

There is *something* for me about that time, when I look

back now. I *know* it was short and that it didn't end the way we hoped, but it was special just the same, I guess *that's* what I'm saying. I *know* that you wanted to just forget it all, right after we left there for the last time. I *know* that you said it was too hard to think about—*I get that,* I really do. At the same time, though, I think I disagree, whether or not I agreed with you back then. I can't remember, but I think about those short moments now, and I just feel warm. *Maybe* it's part of growing or aging or healing, *I don't know,* but I kind of cherish that time now in a way I don't know if you could understand. *Maybe* you could, but I'm not sure. You were in such a hurry to get out of there. You didn't even want to take the scenic route, you just wanted out like it never happened, but, *I don't know,* I feel like those days were good days, I mean, even better than good I guess, they were important, they were necessary.

I don't *know* how to explain it, but I guess *maybe* this is an example: I think about that day we went to *Sunrise Records,* and we were laughing at the combination of the sex toys, the candles, the bongs, and the vinyl albums all in one place. You remember *that* don't you? You thought the picture or mural (or whatever you call a painting like that) on the front wall was majestic. You said you bet it would be a good place to make a baby, and it was hilarious because neither of us ever wanted anything to do with any babies. We were holding hands with Lem in the doorway, I can still feel the touch, and we laughed as we picked out the three records, the one by The Eagles your mother loved, the one by Joni Mitchell because my dad liked her so much, and that Bob Dylan one that we both swore was his best before he did that one with the song "Mississippi." I don't *know* how to put it, but I feel like there was *something* about moments like *that* one that kind of felt more integrated, like we were coming into each other, starting a chapter even if we didn't *know* that yet. There was—how do I put it?—an *opening* there, a small crack in the walls, that let everything since come through, even though leaving felt *so* painful at the time, even though there would be more difficult times.

THE SONG CAME ON AS I PASSED a road called Raleigh on the west side of town—remember we always thought it would be cool to live on the west side when we were kids? We just knew it would be better than the eastside. We just knew it. It really is a beautiful part of town, and if I was thinking about staying here, I think that's where I would probably end up. But I was driving on a road called Hiawassee, past this road called Raleigh and it was like "the perfect storm," (or that's what you would say.) There is a place (not *at*, but *by* that corner) called **JOSIE'S**, and I didn't see what the place does or sells, but right as I saw the sign—Dashboard Confessional's "So Long, So Long" started playing in the car.

I almost drove off the road.

I guess you're right, or I'm right, *we're* right maybe. I guess I am very emotional right now. I haven't thought about Josie in years, I just haven't, it was almost like I *forgot* her somehow. The song started playing, and I *know* you always said I had "way too much" of an emotional reaction to that song, but it started playing and I could see her. I don't mean I was *thinking* about her, necessarily—it was *different*. I could *see* her: three years old in pig tails; seven years old dancing in the grass; twelve years old, climbing the magnolia tree that her mother was allergic to in front of her house; fifteen years old, showing me how to do my makeup that night before we all went out to the party (out in the field on the edge of the park). I could *see* her like she was really there. I could hear her voice. I could feel her laugh. The tears just flooded me. There was no warning. She just came crashing back into my head like she'd always been there, maybe hiding somewhere waiting for the right moment. I lost it. It was 1998 all over again, and I just couldn't breathe or think or anything, much less drive. I pulled into a parking lot with a bar (*The Taproom* or something), a car wash, and a fucking *Dominoes* and just wailed into the steering wheel for what felt like fifteen years or so. How the hell does something like that even happen? What the hell is going on with me? I just don't understand all these feelings.

D O YOU *REMEMBER* WHAT YOUR GRANDMOTHER SAID about the year we were born? She was always saying these oddly comical things that later we would realize were full of all kinds of potential philosophical meanings, *remember?*—as kids we just thought she got a little nutty when she had too many (as she called them) "nips" of whiskey in her Sanka. As the afternoon passed by into the evening she would *forget*.

I think we were ten, but we might have been eleven. We were sitting on that table that wasn't really a table, more like a cut-out in the wall of the house or some kind of desk you might sit *on* because it wasn't being used for writing. (That nook always felt like *I* did in Oviedo, kind of out of place, just *stuck* there for the hell of it for some reason that never seemed to make much sense.) She used it to (as she put it) "throw shit someplace" and sit by the window. (I felt like that too.) She would just talk and talk when she started taking her nips around mid-afternoon, and sometimes there would be stories and tears and laughter and references to old records, some of which we would search for, only to find out they never existed. Other times, like that day at the not-quite-table (or maybe-a-desk) she would just say something that seemed random, that even all these years later I still find myself *thinking* about, probably far more than whiskey-infused words are worth (but there you go, I guess *that,* in and of itself, is a good description of life.)

We were sitting there that day in the year (I can't remember which one it was)—and she said to remember that "there would be things birthed alongside each human that would follow them like a shadow in the background, whether they noticed it or not." She was talking about the factories she grew up walking to with her mama, and later worked at herself, and later watched close down (as the area became more and more destitute and poor), and later would try not to notice, as they decayed, abandoned buildings dotting the edge of town. She was talking about herself.

Maybe it's because we're always getting older, *maybe* it's because we take our own nips these days, but sometimes I wonder if it was a broader statement than simply one about her own life. I mean, well, we were born in the year Reagan rose to office, and we grew up as the free-market, conservative backlash decimated the economy, damn near killed (is still killing) the working class that once existed, and as more and more fights that were supposed to be over seemed to be coming back again and again, and as we still wrestled with the lack of universal health care that even people in the sixties screamed was a problem for a modern nation, and as we continue to depend so much on cars and pollution instead of building a modern transportation network and taking care of our planet.

It also makes me think of something Alex said one morning laughing over tea at that hotel in Atlanta, in College Park, that they said was the best place in the city. They were laughing at people talking about how liberal the '60s and '70s were and how odd the millennials seem to older folk, and someone wanted to know where we all stood. Alex smiled and said they read that we were "the *Oregon-Trail* generation" (like the game *Oregon Trail*) because we had an "analog childhood," in the shadow of the liberal movements of the decades before, and a "digital adulthood" in the shadow of the conservative movements of the eighties and nineties. We were somewhere between "the good old days and the fucked-up present," as they put it, "always out of place, always looking for the next answer" (from both the past and the future generations), which made little sense to us. You and I laughed because we never played *Oregon Trail* (the board game) but we remembered when it showed up in these *new* little boxes called computers, in our classrooms. Alex remembered playing it as a child and then having AOL show up in the nineties in their neighborhood. Alex's friend Kip put it best when she said we were the "lost generation—exactly what happens when you try to make a mashup of a cassette and a CD—never able to be heard fully in any way.

I was *thinking* about these things, and how it seems like our birth created a running soundtrack, at least for me (and probably for others) that I never thought much about, like a radio broadcast or some background programming we only notice at the worst times. I was trying to hear, to feel, the edges of this background, if only for a second, I wanted to taste it. I was sitting in a café in the Kissimmee area of the city, over near all the theme parks where the tourists go to look (and be) miserable as they experience the places supposed to convince them they are happy for a few minutes. I was sitting there thinking about your grandmother telling us she "would never go to those new-fangled parks, not never," as she spilled a sip or nine out of her Sanka, and I heard "Radio Free Europe" playing and thought about us saying R.E.M. was made for us because the band started in 1980 like we did. I remembered how it seemed like every year of my life had an R.E.M. song tied to it, and how you cried a little bit when they retired in 2011.

I didn't have long with these thoughts, though, because the next song that came on reminded me that our soundtrack was fluid or multiple. Next up, the radio played "I Will Follow" by U2 and I started giggling about Donny, who lived around the corner from us, always wanting to play the small instrumental part on the *Boy* cassette for us because he was sure the meaning of life was hidden in that untitled instrumental section somehow. I was smiling about having similar U2 memories throughout our lives after *Boy* came out to meet our birth in 1980 when the radio station (or whatever they're called now that everything is online) shifted to the song "Landlady" off the newly released U2 album, and it hit me that even now they're still following us around.

As the new song played, I thought about the ways we keep coming back to each other after all these years. I thought about the people who have given a hand, a dollar, a random gift to make us smile as we walked such odd paths to make our lives. I think we turned, whether consciously or not, to songs and music because we didn't find a blueprint for what we felt, wanted, and lived in any of the mainstream sources or citations from the churches and the scientists. We saw the cookie-cutter houses and families, but we wanted to roam the world and scream about emotions like Bono or Michael Stipe instead, I guess maybe *that's* what happened. I sat on a wooden bench outside an ice cream parlor in Kissimmee an hour or four later and thought about how little most people and pathways seemed to ever make sense to me. I thought about roaming the country with and without you, somehow always feeling a little of both, and I wondered what might be next, whenever I made sense of this visit home.

WAS DRIVING IN THE NORTHERN PART OF Florida a few weeks before I arrived in the Orlando area. I didn't need to stop on the way, but I did anyway. I stayed at the *Four Points* in Tallahassee, the one that seems ironic because it's a cylindrical building and has no points. I was there wondering if you would come to Florida too, but I was also there remembering too many things at once. Do you remember when Carla used to have a couple free drinks and call me talking about her feelings because she had trouble talking about her feelings when she was sober? I felt like that, but I didn't want to call anyone so instead I just drove around the city (or small town with big colleges that make it seem like a city) each night. I was driving on a one-way street called Sixth Avenue when I saw a sign for CHERRY STREET, and just had to pull off the road and stop for a moment. I sat on the side of Cherry Street in my car for a few minutes, but then I got out and walked the three blocks around Sixth Avenue because something felt right about that.

I was thinking, of course, about our little cottage on Cherry Street. I know, *I know*, I'm sappy and nostalgic and silly—*I get that*, but come on, stick with me for a bit here. I know you say it was just another house in the endless moving that was our life back then, I *know* that, but I always thought it was kind of special. I'm still not sure how we found ourselves in Tennessee in the first place. I really don't know *why* we went to the "House of Love" with Erin that day. She didn't need our help getting out of Alabama, and her grandma didn't even know she was bringing two not-nearly-as-dark-skinned-as-the-rest-of-the-family people along for the ride. But I remember we sat on grandma's porch laughing and cutting up. She called her place the "House of Love" because, she said, "when you got nothing else, well, you can at least afford to have some love in your life, *so*," she said, "this is a place for all that kind of *nonsense* that makes it worthwhile to live through the pain—*you got that kids?*" We got it. Erin's uncle kept coming by every few hours over the three days we were there, and no matter the time of day he was progressively more drunk (or buzzed or whatever)each time, until about nine at night Sunday when, somehow, he just automatically sobered up and said it was work time.

Maybe that's how we ended up on Cherry Street. Maybe we were enchanted by grandma's sense of beauty and adventure in life, by Erin's uncle's lame jokes and desperate attempts to tell us far too much about ducks, *or maybe* we just could relate to Erin running away from her small town of origin in search of grandma's loving arms after a horrid ordeal with parents who just would *not* understand, no matter how hard she tried to get them to do so. I don't *know*, but maybe *something* in there led to the meandering walk through the hills. We were watching the people skateboarding in the tunnels in the mountains, we were thinking they were equally idiotic and brave, and we saw the street sign with the heart sticker on it. It said: CHERRY STR♥. before the heart sticker (that felt bigger than it should have been) cut it off. We all laughed at Josie's obsession with cherries when we were kids, so it felt like a place to walk. We roamed the street, kind of a horseshoe that curved off the main drive but didn't go anywhere (kind of like us and all our travels), and found the cottage with the FOR RENT sign.

It stood there in what Josie would have called a semblance of beautiful, slow, decay.

When we visited the place, we fell in love with the semi-sunken ceilings and the abandoned paddle board. We wondered what someone could have used it for in the mountains. It was just sitting there in the living room, looking like it was uncleaned for far too long, hugging the off-white wall of the house. There was a stain in the middle of the concrete floor of the living room that felt like a scream to another night other people would never forget. There was a lonely two-by-four standing against the window in the back of the room, I felt like it was standing guard; you said it reminded you of something special you couldn't put into words, something only transmitted through touch *or maybe* smell, something you had to feel. I never thought to ask about that later. Maybe I should have. The realtor said the place was rustic, but we thought it felt more like a set of a hollow eyes waiting for the color to come back, hoping the color would come back, wishing to un-see something terribly tragic or wonderfully whimsical *or maybe* a few things that blurred such boundaries.

We moved in that day and started kind of rebuilding the place as an art-studio-meets-hobbit-hole.

Thinking about that place and walking down Cherry Street in Tallahassee, I was met with a memory that seems poignant now though it was probably nothing. You were out doing something, and I came back to the cottage. I walked in the living room. The pink rug we got from the second-hand store covered the old stain, hiding its stories, and the plank of wood still stood against the back wall because you loved it. The paddle board was now a table of sorts we made using other wood around the back of the cottage, and I put my keys on it like I did most days. I was carrying a bag of waffles and I smelled like chicken because that was the result of every day I worked at the chicken shack down the road. I stood there in the middle of the room. I had not yet lit one of the candles we

33

were using until we figured out which lamp to use for light in the main room. Our only real piece of furniture, the bean-bag chair we picked up at a yard sale down the block, sat in all its bright-yellow glory against the edge of the wall beside the CD player that we found at the pawn shop in Alabama where we met Erin.

There was something about that empty room. There was something about the way my eyes scanned left to right to see the newly formed table (made out of the useless-in-this-part-of-the-mountains paddle board) all the way over to the bright-yellow (maybe too bright for even Big Bird to handle), bean-bag bed/chair décor that seemed like home. It was maybe the first time I realized consciously that I'd never known what people meant when they said a place "felt like home" until then. I felt like I could never get close enough to that feeling, and now, on a different Cherry Street in northern Florida years later, before I would talk to you in Orlando about *different ways* people can *miss* things, I finally wanted to understand this thing people call *home*.

I think I'm starting to get a handle on it.

SHE WALKS WITH AN UMBRELLA SWINGING FROM her purse. She works at *Whitney Young* she says—a high school somewhere in this city—as we enter the train on the Blue Line, headed for another part of Chicago, she has an almost senseless grace blended with an almost complete nervousness each time she moves, and somehow it seems like neither the grace nor the nerves come easy for her. She is talking very fast, but she slows each time she says the word "I" and I wonder if those are the moments where her own self, feelings, or thoughts (call it what you want) come out for just a second, just a peek at the world around her.

Every night we sit together in hard-but-not-too-hard orange seats and the train lurches off into the night. She is talking about reading in bed. She is talking about missing someone or something that seems to matter. She is talking very fast, except whenever she uses the word "I" for the next thirty minutes on the train.

We get off the train at Jackson and switch to the Red Line. We move in pace with the other strangers. She stops to give some cash to the guy sitting in the hallway. The station is loud, more alive than most of America feels, with sounds and shapes and colors and feelings and bodies all rhythmically working together. "It's like a dance club" (she said on another night) "the lack of these places in our country is probably why people go to dance clubs so much and get so smashed in hopes of touching or feeling or experiencing other people just like this for a few hours." (I don't *know* if she's right, but I don't *care.*)

We get on the Red Line train. We are headed north where the crowd gets whiter and whiter with each stop (the same way there are more varied and darker skintones on the train if you go south on the Red Line.) We pass the usual stops. We don't notice. She is talking about work. She likes her job, but people annoy her. She is talking about school. She is about to have a graduate degree, but now everyone else seems stupid to her. Everyone has always seemed stupid to *me,* so I kind of *get that.* The sound of ringing bells accompanies us as we get off at our stop and step into the station where we first met a few weeks prior.

It was late at night. She was coming back from her movie-night-with-friends. I was lost, having just arrived in the city a few nights before that. I had been trying to find a used-books bookstore near the Argyle exit that I never found. All these years later, I wonder if it ever existed at all. I was standing on the platform (as I learned to do in other cities with actual transportation systems); I was nervous because I was lost. I was staying in *The Loop*, as they called it. She was coming back

35

from a movie night. She later told me they were watching sappy films somewhere near Clarendon and Lawrence, but I didn't recognize the street names. I didn't know where that was. We were at the Wilson stop. We didn't know each other then. We were just on the platform at the same time. It was a cold night. There was a guy (there *always* is, I guess) who just *had* to experience his intoxication by bothering me. He kept trying to talk to me. I didn't want to talk. He kept trying to touch me. I didn't want to be touched. I was backing away. I was trying to avoid him. He didn't want to be avoided. I was trying to calmly get out of the situation, flashing back to others like it. He didn't want to be calm. I was scared. He was cursing. I felt cold. He smelled like a liquor store.

I don't *know* how it happened (it was so long ago, but *that's* no excuse, my memory is usually great, but I don't *know* how it happened)—it just did. I remember suddenly seeing long, rather attractive, shapely legs with stockings covering them (I must have been looking down, frozen in a pose meant to suggest I wanted to be left alone, I wanted to disappear)—the stockings were shiny—I saw an umbrella dangling from a purse, a long coat like I imagined fancy women wore when out at night (not the kind I could afford)—moving in black shadows. I don't *know* what she said. I looked up—*I remember that.* From the hemline I followed the long coat up to her kind-of-somewhere-between-long-and-short, brown hair, and I saw her reach out a long, slender finger, the kind that could command armies, into the face of the man who wanted my attention, or my body (*it was hard to tell*). She put her finger within an inch of his eye. Her other hand balled into a fist at first, but then it opened, and I swore she used it to motion for me to get behind her. I did. I saw her nod slightly as she told him to stop. Her voice was iron. It wasn't like the blend of nervousness and grace I would come to know was her usual. It was hard. It was without equivocation. It was *absolute* in the silence of the late-night station.

He didn't want to take her seriously. He tried to reach

for her. She moved back but kept her finger in his face and said something I didn't catch in that hard, cold voice-that-is-not-the-voice-she-normally-has-when-she-talks-about-movie-nights-or-reading-in-bed. I was scared, but I was feeling much less cold despite the temperature. I was standing behind her following her motions. She used the second hand to keep track of where I was. When she stepped back, I did too. When she stepped forward into his face again, with more frightening words coming out of her mouth again a few seconds later, I followed her. He took her seriously this time. I saw fear, like I'd felt, flash in his eyes. His eyes were afraid. I will never understand it, but he looked at me as if *I* would help *him* against this well-dressed, beautiful woman who seemed ready to cut him from groin to grin.

He started backing away.

His hand started shaking and he moved away from her.

He muttered, "*bitch.*"

Whipping her body around—faster than I would have thought smart on a cold, rainy night, on a patch of concrete high above the roads—she faced me. She wanted to know if I was *okay*. I was not, but I *was* at the same time. She said her name was Ellen, I said my name was Millie. She said we should get on the train together when the next one came to the station. I said thank you. I was choking up. She asked if she could hug me. I said yes. She hugged me on the platform. She kept her arm around me on the train ride. I felt warm again. She talked a little about the asshole, "the latest asshole" as she put it (and I saw it) on the platform, but more so, she started talking about her life and her movie night. I just wanted to hear her talk. It made me feel safe then and made me feel happy long after. She offered to walk me home. I didn't want her to see the broken-down hovel I was renting. I felt like her coat would hate it, and then me. She told me to text her, so she knew I got home okay. I did. It was nice that someone cared.

I don't *know* why I just shared all *that* with you again. I know you already knew that story. I *know* we've talked about it before, but, *I don't know*, it felt important to say it again. I guess sometimes we need to repeat things to see if we understand them better or learn again from them or just to share with someone we know will give a damn. I guess it is also because *that* time, not like the others, but *that* time in Chicago reminds me of *this* time in Orlando. It was another time when you were distant. It was another time when I didn't see you as much. It was another time when I missed you a lot as I was trying to figure things out. *Maybe that's* why I went for the repeat above—*maybe that's it. Maybe* sometimes we go back into this or that story as a way to talk about something we're feeling that we don't know exactly how to (or if) we should or could express. *Maybe* I'm just making excuses, "making up the why's" as you would say, but it feels *right*. I guess I just miss you even more tonight, and it *is* unusually cold in Orlando, so I thought about that night on the platform when I felt cold and alone until I met Ellen.

THERE WAS A DECK THAT YOU LOVED so much on the backside of the property at the house in Thomasville, Georgia. Remember we lived in the extra room the young Jewish couple had for rent, and we would walk along the lake for hours when we had days off from the coffee shop downtown. It is still funny to think of that small patch of shops as downtown, but funny or not, that was what it was called. We would sit out on the old deck staring into the water. Do you remember the sweet young woman who owned the house worrying about us because, as she put it, the *old* deck was not exactly "finished with its part in the renovation process grasping the entire house" while we were there? There was the other deck, the new one we saw other people use, but the busted one with the creaky wood, splinters, and missing second rail seemed to fit us better.

We were always like that, your mom even said so when we were little. We wouldn't go first to the new section of the cassettes (and later CDs)—nope, not us, we hit the bins and wanted the ones that were pre-loved by someone else. We would do the same with clothes. We would do the same with so many stereos over the years. We did it with everything. We still do. We somehow find beauty in the discarded things of others, and in so doing, make them new, I would say, but I don't *know* where that came from initially even if I think about it. I mean, we had new things *and* hand-me-downs from our family growing up, but they aspired to *only* have new things—even though that was impossible for them in the post-Reagan U.S. (whether or not it ever would have been possible before that, we didn't know). We sought to repurpose as many discarded things as we could, even when we were too small to give a damn about the economy, much less about buzz words like "retro," "chic," or anything of the sort. I wonder *why*—like I always do—but I have no clue. I know that later it was at least as much out of necessity as love—we were poor and roaming the country from town to town, never quite staying long enough to make any real money beyond the minimum wage- and tip-based jobs we could get. We did what we could with such limited resources.

I think it goes back to leaving Orlando and Oviedo in a sea of taillights, without much of a plan, in the middle of the night, in 1998. I didn't think I would ever come back, but I guess if I was going to, twenty years later makes the most sense. What was it you always said, "life is about *disappearing* and *reappearing* at the most appropriate times," or something like that? You always say things far better than I can, but I try, and you find it cute, so I guess that's good enough for me. I do think it goes back to that first get-out-of-town-as-fast-as-we-can experience. We never bothered to look into the future. I guess that means it also makes sense that in the end (so far at least—*right?*) I came back to the past when I ran out

39

of ideas about where to run next. *Maybe* the answers I've been so desperate to find have always been here, but of course, I *know* you would tell me that there are no answers, only whatever I'm willing to believe.

Yeah, I *know*—*I get that*, you agnostic you . . . *la la la*, whatever—*I get that*, but I guess I just wish I could feel like I really *know* something for sure, some kind of certainty, some kind of understanding, just to hold onto at night. And no, before you say it, I'm not trying to become one of those theists or atheists, and you should know (I've told you before) your jokes about *me* becoming one of those believers are not nearly as funny as you think they are. The ways we have fun watching the atheists squirm whenever we point out how similar their own "beliefs" (*ooh*, they *hate* that word, *don't they?*) are to the theists'—those moments are truly hilarious, I admit that, and it's why I play along in those cases. *Maybe* we have something in common with the atheist folks, *maybe that's* what they did, they recycled something that wasn't working anymore into a similar version of the same thing they could call their own. *Maybe that's* what their faith is, it's like our stereos—same parts just a new name and new owners. I guess I can understand *that* even if I think they're silly for saying they "*believe* stuff but are not religious because they believe the truth" (you know, like the Baptists say) "so it's not the same."

Okay, I admit it, I did that thing you always say I do. I got sidetracked, but *maybe* it fits or something. I was trying to figure out why I was thinking about that old deck and religion in the first place, and I think it was because I saw this woman walking by wearing a shirt just like the one our landlady wore all the time at that house in Thomasville. You *remember* that shirt?—you *know* you do. It was perfect, smartass, and beautiful. The one I saw earlier had an orange background instead of purple, but it worked just as well, and the phrase was the same: **GOT CHUTZPAH**. I guess that led me back to our days on the deck, the same way everything these days seems to lead me back to one of our travels or another.

I do wonder if it is just an *aging* thing, all this reflection and revisiting our origins, but I also wonder if it's something more. You said that I was in trouble when I started sleeping with *them*. You know who I mean, of course, it has been a couple years now since that day they touched my hand in some magical way in that garage for the fancy cars, *so maybe* it's about *them*. Is that what you meant about "*missing* people," at the park behind the *Park Avenue Records* store that night? *I don't know.* It feels like I might be right and wrong at the same time. Is this about *them*? Is this about *us*? Is it about *me*? I don't *know*. I can't tell yet, so I *know* you would say I have more thinking to do—*I get that*, I'm not complaining, and I'll do it. I just wish it made sense for me, like it all seems to for you. Why can't I *get* that?

Y OU MIGHT FIND IT SURPRISING, BUT I'VE BEEN THINKING about daddy a lot lately. I remember when we were passing through Mississippi one of those times, I kept saying that I wanted to think of him as the main character in the Drive-by Truckers song "Where the devil don't stay," but you said he was more likely a "Bob." As you know, I never knew much about him or how he got to Oviedo from Beaumont in the first place. I *do* know: he was here for a few years, at least (because he met mama); "they *accidentally*," as she always stressed when she was drinking, "*made* me;" and then he worked over at one of the parks for a while. I know that he was known as an angry drunk, a belligerent person that almost no one could be around for very long, and the kind of man who was always desperate to prove to other men that he was, in fact, a man. He was what Margo would say was "a person suffering from chronic insecurity" that he couldn't help but unleash on the rest of the world every chance he got.

You *remember*? I didn't even blink much when mama

41

slipped up on my fifteenth birthday and suggested daddy wasn't *daddy*. "It could have been that nice bisexual fella who ran off up north, now that I think about it," she slurred over her always-present, West-Palm-Beach, coffee cup that held the always-present mixture of coffee and very, very heavy liquor. *Remember?*—we joked that we knew it was a bad day when she was just walking around the house (before we went to school) with that big vodka bottle and one of the t-shirts daddy left her (the closest thing to child support she ever got from him. I didn't even blink. I think in some ways I was kind of relieved to have another option. I didn't even care if the-fella-who-ran-off-up-north was an *asshole* too, I could imagine him any way I wanted to, and I remember I settled on a male version of Lucinda Williams. That was all I ever needed from either of the-daddies-I-never-met, some kind of origin story for my own southern gothic shitshow of a life.

Anyway, I *know* this is all old news, but really, what isn't old news after all the time we've spent together?—*you know?*—it's not like there's anything about our surface-level information we don't already know. What I wanted to say was simply that I find myself thinking about him more and more lately. I wonder if life would have been different (even though likely worse) if I met him. I wonder where he went next on his own life of skipping from town to town. I wonder if he left any other drunk women, "drunken angels" (as my mother liked to call herself when she was trying to karaoke that song at the dive bar over off Colonial in East Orlando) and "damned accidents" (as she so often referred to me). I wonder if he ever stopped running. I wonder if he ever found anything worth running *to* instead of *from*.

I guess it's because ever since that day in the garage with the fancy cars, I guess I've been wondering so much about my own running (past and present). I'm trying to figure out if I'm running *from* them or running so I can come back *to* them. You know better than anybody how freaked out I was when I just shut down on Alex that night in the apartment by the

Waffle House. I don't *know* what happened, and I still don't even *remember* that night in full. You said "it wasn't pretty," but you wouldn't tell me anything else. You said I "couldn't handle *knowing*," and that's why I don't remember. I think it was about Alex specifically, but maybe it was about *everything*— between *us* leaving here, and *me* running into Alex. I don't *know*, but I wonder if *daddy* is part of the answer or part of whatever problem I might have, or whatever it is that keeps me running. I don't *know*. I guess I'll have think on that, but I've had about sixteen *Not Your Father's Root Beer*s and I can barely see anything right now.

DID YOU EVER THINK ABOUT THE **PATHS** we drove over the years? I *know* you don't like to have plans or feel tied down by anything, but I often wondered. *Remember* when you used to collect all those maps? You would mark up all the places you have been with yellow tacks, and mark up all the places you might go with red tacks, and mark up some places you would like to go with green tacks—*do you remember that?* They were such simple things, those road maps we picked up for nickels (sometimes for free) at side-of-the-road gas stations and diners. I was looking at one earlier today that was sitting on the table I chose at the *Starbucks*. I wondered if maybe you were there before me, and you were charting your next adventure. That made me wonder if you had ever charted *any* of them, or if it was all just random, driving to wherever- no-one-knew-us-yet. I admit that was my own approach over the years, but I wonder about you.

I was thinking about these things while sipping my coffee. I still drink the same mixture of coffee with what you call "the wrong kind of milk" and what you call "that yucky raw sugar." I *know* you know this, but I thought *reading* it might make you laugh. I always try to make you laugh. Margo worried for a while that I wasn't able to laugh—*remember* that?—because we have that thing where the weight of the years feels heaviest on the lips. Sometimes smiles are like trying to climb a mountain that people go to when seeking to say goodbye to the world via an attempt at cliffdiving. The muscles just don't seem to want to work, and it gets to be *so* normal not to smile (*remember you said this?*) that the rare occasion where you smile naturally surprises you, almost like you forgot you knew how to do it— or forgot what it *meant* in the first place. Margo said that she thought "whatever passed for life was a little like a marathon, based on who could forget the most for the longest—in order to want to keep living."

I miss Margo sometimes. I heard she bought a house with Dana somewhere in Indiana a couple years ago. If I was the type to keep in touch with anyone (well anyone other than *you* and I guess You-Know-Who nowadays) I would send a card or one of those online messages I don't understand (but I doubt I'll ever do that).

I was thinking about *memory* as I looked over the surprise map. I was wondering if I could remember all the mean highways and creepy two-lane roads we traveled. I found myself tracing our path from the I-4 corridor to northwestern Florida. It felt comforting, so I kept going, at first (just for a little while, I told myself) but then I was moving down I-10 into Alabama, Mississippi, and Louisiana. You remember, though, of course, we got bored with I-10, despite taking so many back roads. We were bored so we went into Northern Louisiana and into Arkansas and then even into Oklahoma. We hit Missouri, Indiana, and Illinois before heading back east that first time. We were like radio waves, transmitting ourselves across the country, bouncing along black tops, between the mountains, along the coast. Then, we spent some time "missing out on as much as possible in Ohio," as you put it, then did Pennsylvania and New York and wound our way through the northeast until we spent those two weeks that summer in Boothbay Harbor, Maine. I don't remember how we left, but it was separately.

You said you went out west, and I went down the east coast. I passed through the I-95 corridor checking out small towns here and there along the way. I found myself just on the edge of Savannah *(remember I wrote you about that weekend?)* and headed into Atlanta, then Birmingham, then I was going to Mobile until you showed up in Birmingham, telling me wild stories about shit that you swore you somehow heard about *my* travels on the east coast. Then you told me some crazier shit about a dragon that got loose somewhere in North Alabama, and I just about died laughing. You said *that* was the problem. People were so closed minded that no one was likely to report the story and keep everyone prepared for the *next* time a dragon went drunkenly roaming through the south. I told you to shut up. You said we needed cash. I had that bracelet leftover from the jewelry we found in that abandoned building we slept in, back when we were in Carbondale, Illinois. We pawned it and met Erin, right as she was headed for Tennessee, so we went too—you *terrified* the whole time we would accidentally cross paths with that silly dragon you made up for some reason.

We kept going and going even after that. We crisscrossed the east side of the country, and even made it out west a few times together later, even as our ages continued to rise. *Remember* when we met that guy in Morgan, Utah?—who was so afraid to be free that he would fight anyone, anyway he could, who even (for a second) challenged his own beliefs about just how *absolute,* "godly" (as you put it) and *true* all science just *had* to be? We'd spent most of the night making him almost cry by pointing out all the shit that science has gotten wrong over time, and reminding him that science so far had not even been able to discover the existence of many different types of *people* because it was too busy pretending math, two sexes only, and other silly, limited, binary ideas were really *Oh-My-God* and really *True* (because Jesus-but-not-Jesus, or maybe Darwin, *said* so), despite all the evidence to the contrary. I remember you were about to spit out your drink when you realized the

45

guy was once a Mormon because you found it so hilarious that someone would leave one fundamentalist religion only so he could form his own around another set of leaps of faith and sacred texts (*that* probably wasn't the most fun memory from out west, but it always sticks in my head.)

By the time I looked at the map in a more serious way, a couple hours after I started, I realized that I had colored in so much it was hard to tell where we *hadn't* been yet. My pen marks were everywhere. I didn't notice it at first, but, since I went in order, there were lines upon lines upon lines at some points, while there were other parts of the map that got more singular treatment. I stared at the map for more time than seemed necessary, formulating something. I ignored the Jackson Garner and Casey Plett novels sitting beside it.

The map was everything. Each line had a story about us, but nowhere could I find or remember a place we ever seemed to fit. It was "the kind of thought, or realization" as mom would say, "that was both happy and sad." Maybe *that's* why I thought of the binary- and other truth-obsessed guys in Utah. We just never seem to *fit* anywhere in the categories presented, and so much of life just won't fit into an either/or description.

I feel like I always knew this on some level, but *maybe* you're rubbing off on me and I'm beginning to be able to put such things into words.

"TELL ME THE TRUTH ABOUT DOLPHINS," said the little girl with the pig tails moving across a swimming sea of people in the Florida Mall. The child looks the way the posters suggest she should look: brimming eyes, trembling lips, a bit of maybe a brownie still clinging to her left cheek, more words than her mouth can hold, spilling out all over the place, simply thrilled. The lights are everywhere. There is a shop full of people and crayons that blend light and color in an odd way as people create their custom sets that may or may not become part of an amazing art project or maybe a forgotten memory in the bottom of a cedar chest. Six kids run together, to the alarm of at least seven adults they pass, chasing freedom between the shoppers and yelling at each other about the *Old Navy* store they believe their supervisors, caregivers, or whatever you want to call them, are in at the moment. It is on the other side of the massive mall. I wonder if they know that or even care. They look too happy to care, and I hope they are.

Maybe we're also the mall generation or *maybe* it's just part of the "never-fitting-in thing" that us folks with only *Oregon Trail* in common experience, but as you *know*, I've always enjoyed roaming around malls watching the people, enjoying and feeling saddened by what appears to always be the exact same stores in every one of them. Like we did in Houston, and in Chicago on that mile people think nicely of, and even in the middle of nowhere in some town called Kokomo (like in the Beach Boys song you like—but really in the middle of the cornfields of Indiana), I'm walking around the mall today to clear my head. I still do this whenever it's too cold outside for me and my Florida-crafted bones to take my walks outdoors. You asked me years ago what it was about malls that I liked so much, and I couldn't answer. I was never that good at putting things into words before Alex got a hold of me in that parking garage a couple years ago, but I think I figured it out and would like to share. Maybe then at least one part of this transmission will be something new or interesting. Yes, I still worry about boring you, and yes, I *know* you think that's cute. And yes, I still think your fondness for my insecurity is strange.

I was thinking about it as I parked outside the Sears here at the Florida Mall. There was a song playing on the stereo in my car. I think it was a pop hit from 2014 (or 2011) that I blared when Alex and I were having trouble and you were telling me to be patient); it was a song about someone named Lily, and I was thinking about the day Mattie came down from up north to look after me when I called out for help. I was blaring this song Lily song and I was trying to wake up, metaphorically *and* physically I guess, and Alex was coming down for a visit and I was scared because I didn't know what was going on—*remember?* You were making coffee while Mattie was in the shower, and you said you couldn't understand why I kept playing this song, but you admitted you never liked the band too much in the first place. You said it was like you loved them the first couple times you heard each song. You said the flourishes and sing-along quality made you feel, but then it wore away and felt just repetitive. The song repeated on my computer stereo in the small apartment in Atlanta. Mattie was singing some other pop song that felt like 2017 or maybe 2009 as they emerged from the bathroom with towels for clothes.

Anyhow, that same Lily song was playing as I got out of the car beside the Sears sign. It made me think, *you know?* it made me pause. You, of course (I even admitted it then) were *right* about that particular band. Flourishing pop hooks and lazy, repetitive, emotional lyrics are the template, and it does work so well getting the feelings going before feeling repetitive. The exception, I think, and even *you* said so one time after six or eight rum-and-cokes loosened you up at that sports bar with the signs about the **BULLS** and where they should start. You were obsessed with those signs on the strips of tape on the floor (we never found the bulls). Anyhow, the exception, I think, is that one song about the "Sixteen-ounce monster" because that song just never seems old. But as the song about Lily played it hit me that I could understand malls the same kind of way I explained my interest in this song to you all those years ago. "It was a similar kind of thing," as Josie always said. The songs are repetitive, but when you're feeling what they're about, like me with the Lily song, they feel so fresh, so poignant, and the repetition speaks to you on some deep level. I think malls are the same way. They're repetitive, and they look and seem basically the same wherever you go. They're the ultimate example of just how conformist and religious our nation really is—everyone buys the same brands in the same enclosed space surrounded by the same people you will not touch, know, or speak to in any way unless you absolutely have to: these are the rules. But as Ellen noted, "there are so few places where we are all together in the heat, sweat, awkwardness, and chaos that nature seems to thrive on" (and we all seem to desire for some reason). Maybe the malls, like the nightclubs, give us a safe, controlled version of human contact we can cling to without changing anything significant in our lives. It is repetitive, and that can get old, but it is also speaking to something deep inside of us, some desire to be with other people even if we hate them, and that makes it poignant, like the Lily song for me or any pop song people love.

I think that is why I like the malls. You can watch people watching each other. You see people longing to connect and doing so in whatever limited ways they feel safe or comfortable doing: The man cracking jokes no one wants to hear with the salespeople; the woman talking to strangers about her job and how it makes her feel, knowing she won't have to put up with these people ever again; the children running wild and asking strangers awkward questions—you see people slamming into each other the ways they feel comfortable doing so in our culture while leaving enough room to go back to their silos afterward. You also see the pain in the isolation, the symptoms of being *Alone with Everybody* that Richard Ashcroft sang about so long ago, remember how much you and Margo loved that album? You two were playing it nonstop for a while there in our twenties.

You see the people stick to their little packs, like animals lost in the woods. You see them pay for more than they need as if they are searching for something that will speak to them, the way another human might be able to in a better moment.

You see the dirty looks children and lovers receive from so many adults wearing sad and tired eyes for demonstrating freedom and emotion and joy in forms of affection, play, and humor. The mall is one of those places where pleasure and pain collide in brief, passing glances and bodily twitches. On a more practical level, of course, and I'm sure you've been saying it in your head while reading this, yes, I really wanted some of that teriyaki rice I love, and I'll sit here in the food court now and eat a big Styrofoam box of it, thank you very much.

DO YOU EVER THINK ABOUT THE LADY with the psychic shop that had all the stereotypical ingredients of such a shop from the movies as well as a random, pink, Chicago Cubs hat when we landed in that store trying to escape the rain in Nashville that one night? I don't think she got a lot of business in general as she seemed surprised to see us or anyone at all, but she had this hearty laugh and a habit of tapping her left pinkie finger on the table as she spoke. She thought you were some kind of magic that invaded my brain for good and bad reasons. She thought I was "a little nutty," she said, "but nutty in the fun artistic way rather than the creepy, *Criminal Minds* episode kind of way." She talked about how important names were for a while there when you were looking at the candles. She said she left Chicago for Nashville because her mama was always a fan of Dolly Parton. She said she got on a bus and learned the importance of names right away as her own adventures began in the summer of 1979.

She was on the bus headed for Nashville, but she said she didn't know there was a Nashville in Indiana and was surprised to find herself there later in the day. As luck would have it, she enjoyed the writing of Don Pendelton at the time, and she arrived just in time to pick up a copy of his latest book,

Monday's Mob, which spends some time discussing Nashville, Indiana. A woman with a heart for animals, she also spent some time at the Reptile Kingdom that was once a mainstay of the tiny, and I do mean tiny (*remember* we looked the place up after meeting her?) town in the middle of something a little less fascinating than nowhere. She said "it taught her an important lesson." She said you had to "know how to name what you wanted, where you wanted to go, and what you wanted to find." She said if you couldn't at least do that, you had no hope in finding your destination "no matter how brave or cunning you might be." As she sat in her shop in the Nashville most of us have heard of already, she said that other Nashville with its cute side streets and historic districts and as-famous-as-small-towns-can-be-I-guess artist colony showed her the importance of asking "what if" and doing the data analysis to answer such questions rather than simply blindly running for anything at the origin of a simple idea.

I was thinking about this as I passed another psychic shop, just as stereotypical-looking (but no Cubs hat, I checked) in the International Drive area of town where so many tourists spend their nights and days when they come here trying to escape the names, towns, and histories that make up their own lives. The people in this shop were not as talkative (or maybe as bored) as you thought she was *and maybe* why she talked with us for three hours without charging us any money for the advice. There were customers smiling and giggling among themselves about the tie-dye shirts and Grateful Dead bears that seem to populate such spaces, and it reminded me of the little shop called *Rosie's* we found on the edge of Augusta, Georgia all those years ago. I was looking at a t-shirt that said, "**WEST PALM READINGS***" and then on the back, beside a matching asterisk, it said, "***FREE BAGEL WITH FALSE PROMISES FOR EACH CUSTOMER**." I was smiling at the ways we use names to signify all kinds of things that may be inside (or better-known) jokes about experiences, places, relationships, and what not.

It made me think about the way you said we *missed* each other but in *different* ways. It made me think about the idea of *missing* someone. It's a phrase that's used so often that I wonder *how often* anyone thinks to ascertain the *meaning* of it. What does it *mean*, I wonder, when people say they *miss someone, something*, or *anything?* When I think about *missing you*, for example, it is not the *same* way I *miss* Alex or Mattie right now. It is not the *same* way I *miss* Jeff or Cole or Tylor or Ellen or even Pink right now. I *miss* each of them in similar and different ways to each other, to you, and I guess to other things. I even find it amazing as I sit here that I *miss* so many people, I would not have expected *that* to ever happen, and I bet it surprises you too. For *so* long, I mean, we only seemed to have each other and our travels. For *so* long, that was, *hell, we* were all we had to hang on to for dear life.

When I think about *missing* the important people (you and the others) I think about a visceral ache, a need that never seems to satiate or go away, even if I am able to be around each of you repeatedly or for long periods of time. It feels like a part of *me* is missing, a part that might be better than the sum of the rest of the parts. It feels like one of those accordion folders your mother liked to keep documents in when we were young. I was flat on the outside, in appearance, but each of you opened up new compartments inside me, and once these compartments were open, I wanted (like nothing I ever needed before) to find ways to keep them open, to make it easier whenever I needed to reach into them to recall something important (the same way Mom would reach in for a birth certificate at the beginning of the school year). When I go too long without reaching in the compartments, I feel like I'm going flat again, just a folder that has no use, in a cosmic sense, I guess, and that aches in ways that would not have been nearly as conscious to me when I felt like I really was all alone in the world. I don't *know* if any of this makes any sense, but I'm still trying to understand how we might miss each other *differently.*

I WAS TRYING TO MAKE SENSE OF

APPEARANCE AND *disappearance*. I was sitting in a chair with graffiti on it, at the *Drunken Monkey* coffee house on Bumby, despite not being in the mood for a vegan or gluten-free vegan brownie today, (miracles never cease) and sipping a mocha because I felt in need of a treat for some reason that is likely not important. You appeared in a dream and in the living room this morning. You were soft and affectionate the way you always seem to know how to be, like when we were cuddled up together in the sand on the beach of Hilton Head Island, listening to "The One I Love" and making fun of fire with our own little pseudo lyrics under the stars that looked pink that night. You were whispering, the way you do, in my ear all the time when you want to watch me shiver and touching my face with only three of the fingers on your right hand, a pattern I noticed long ago and asked about so many times.

Sometimes I go back in my mind to relive those moments. Do you *remember* the field with the sunflowers and tulips on the edge of town when we were teenagers? We wrapped ourselves in that blanket (the one with the cartoon characters on it that you got, then lost, then recently got again) because Alex wanted you to have another one to make you smile. We watched the stars. They were singing. We could hear it even if no one else could. I remember the trembling of your lips. I remember you started singing or whispering (or whatever) lyrics from "With or without you" and later I told you that I felt like there were dancers in the sky picking out the songs that popped into our heads whenever we spent nights like that in the field. I remember every scent, every touch, every smile, every giggle, and every time we tried to hide the red patterns blushing our faces whenever we tried to be sweet despite the urge to hide vulnerability. I remember these things, but not just that, I *feel* them.

I was thinking about a different one of these nights sitting on the graffiti, and it was almost like what you would call fate, after of course reminding me you are not superstitious as if I would ever forget anything about you, because there was a person who walked into the coffee house, passing just in front of where I was sitting on the sidewalk or porch or whatever you would call that small stretch by the doorway at the *Drunken Monkey*, and they were wearing a shirt with a life guard stand on it, and my computer suddenly picked that moment to play "Dashboard Confessional," and as if that wasn't enough, my email noticed I was in Orlando and adjusted my concert updates to tell me Dashboard was playing nearby in a couple weeks after I thought they retired. I was washed over by all these pieces of what you called "emotional currency," and I found myself replaying in my mind the conversation when you said "So Long, So Long" wasn't really a sad song, it was a song about longing for something and loving someone whether or not you could ever touch them, it was a song about the longevity of real connection, and after you spoke you ran your hands through my hair, kicked a rock into that river we were standing by under another set of dancing stars, and yelled one last time before our twenties were over.

I was flooded with the *reappearance* of these memories and with an almost-empty cup of mocha. I thought about the ways we *appear* to each other at first and how often the *disappearance* of that initial impression is what leads to a deeper, lasting connection and the *reappearance* of people in our lives in pleasant ways. I was thinking about you telling me how you first thought I was kind of an *asshole* as a little kid because I was so full of myself on the ball field and so quiet, like I hated everyone, off the field. I was thinking about how you loved and hated this version of what I might be at the same time, enough to talk to me, and how you found it fascinating that I was really just scared, wishing for relief from a life that already didn't seem to fit right, and too nervous to ever know what to say. I was thinking about how this pattern of impression, giving way to reality, shows up in so many relationships.

It reminded me of reading one of the novels by Patricia

Leavy, where she played with impression versus reality in the case of people from different economic backgrounds. That, of course, made me think of Alex. Alex somehow saw me, the actual me, better than anyone else could from the beginning, but even they ran into misperceptions of things that I find cute to this day. I remember they thought I was aloof, less emotional, and kind of casual about them, probably their own feelings playing hell with them, the way my own do *me*, and your own do *you*, and everyone else as well, I guess, but in reality, I was so overwhelmed by them that I had trouble breathing or speaking whenever they were near. Now, I was never all that good of a speaker anyway, but it was especially odd to not even be able to put two or three words together. They thought I was aloof, but I was *terrified* out of my head. They understand that so well now, but I smile at the time it took for me to show them.

I was also thinking about the ways we think our lives will go versus the ways they end up going. Do you *remember* when we met Mattie, for example? At that point, we had a commitment to form no connections at all to anyone. We were already fighting about letting Cole get close to us, and we were certain that connections were dangerous, constant traveling or running or "moving," as you would say, *that* was our safety valve, and connections could muck that up in intolerable ways. Mattie had no clue about me, *remember?*—he thought I was this worldly expert who knew everything and could teach him about the world. He thought I was invincible, devoid of the kind of pain he was feeling from that traumatic experience he had as a teenager a few years before we met. He thought I had all the answers, and it was only later, especially after he partly broke my heart by lying to me at a time when I was (for some reason) trusting him, that he realized I had what you and Alex call "a gooey, emotional center hidden deep inside the shell" that protects me against this life. My "invincibility," as he said later, "is a mask" I wear to survive. I like that idea, but I don't *know* if it is correct, and I guess it doesn't matter.

YOU SHOULD BE SO PROUD OF ME right
NOW. I'm just kidding, but not really, *but maybe*, I'm not
sure. That sounded so much cuter in my head, and now
I'm trying to decide if I should delete it and maybe even the
whole letter and start over. *Damn*, as Mattie calls it, "anxiety
brain" just messing with me, I hope, so I'll just keep going.
But, all joking aside, you will be pleased (or whatever you
will be) to know that I finally made it into Oviedo. I *know*—
right?—it only took me so damn long to drive that far east, but
what was it Cole always said?—"you gotta take even the small
victories wherever they come from and however you get them."
I'm going with that today.

I decided that the first thing on my Oviedo reunion tour
should be the diner we thought was so cute when we were kids.
I can hear your mouth watering right now over the pancakes at
Town House, water away baby, they still are amazing, though
I only found out for *you*—as we both know, I would rather be
munching on luscious waffles instead, but "we make sacrifices
for the ones we love," as Margo used to say. Sacrifice, that's
what it feels like to go to a diner without waffles—you *know* I'm
telling you the truth on this point. I can see you laughing right
now and remembering me whining about it as a kid. The place
has changed a lot in twenty years, and it is still kind of hard to
believe the place has been around since the 1950's. These days,
for however long—I have no clue as I didn't feel like asking
lots of questions today—they even have a little rainbow flag
sidewalk (that made me smile) out in the front of the shopping
center, well, it is kind of on the side, but same idea. I thought
about going other places while I was there because I finally
made it, "got up the nerve," you would say, but I felt a little
overwhelmed in *Town House*, so I just watched the people. I
remember Josie said it was one of the best places to just see
people, and I guess I was channeling her.

There was this older couple sitting behind me, and I kept
shifting in my seat to look at them without seeming odd for
looking at them. They reminded me of so many people I've seen

over the years, but there was something about two people in maybe their seventies laughing over the "funny pages," as your mom would call them, "those silly cartoons," as mom would call them, in the booth of a diner without a care in the world. They were talking about their son Terry who just married the love of his life Gary, and I thought the rhyming names sounded so cute for some reason I can't truly express. It reminded me of the time Cole and I were in the diner with the vegan cookies and we just listened, stopped everything we were doing really, when that elder lesbian couple told anyone who would listen about their wonderful daughter who was graduating college and how much fun they were having visiting on such a special occasion. There was, I guess, something peaceful about it, something I think would have been nice to see or hear or know about when we were here as kids, *something* like that.

There was what looked like a mid-thirties couple on the other side of the restaurant. They had that thing some people have where it seems like every movement is coordinated even though it really could not have been. The one that seemed more masculine was so small that it was amazing to watch them devour a salad that seemed so large to my eyes. The more feminine one kept smiling at their partner, watching them eat the massive salad, and listening to them talk about some ongoing quest (the kind that only makes sense inside the jokes and habits of a relationship) to try all the Greek salads in the world. It looked like they could have been anywhere, not just in any diner, *anywhere,* and I thought about the Greek salad we loved at the *Landmark Diner* in Atlanta, and I kept smiling because I could not tell if they were a new relationship or had been together decades because they were so much in sync, yet so affectionate and caring that it somehow felt like it could have been both of these things at once. It was the kind of image you think would make a better card than anything Hallmark has ever come up with that I have seen, like, a real picture of love in action. It reminded me of one of those love songs Alice Cooper did in the eighties, though it's hard to remember exactly which one. I always thought it would be sweet to cover one of those for someone special, just for fun.

On the other side of the restaurant, there was also one of your favorite things about contemporary society: a person (who knows what gender if any) with purple hair and a tattoo of a piano, and another that said **LIKE INK**—laughing over some fancy kind of toast with another person who looked masculine but had more feminine mannerisms—eating a plate of eggs and smiling with very soft eyes. It was strange because it was almost like the one with the eggs had both the face of a criminal and the eyes of a poet, and it was almost like the one with the toast had this air of artistry about them, a soft and hard kind of essence that suggested both severe concerns and endless optimism. *Maybe* I was reading into them too much, or *maybe* they just kind of captivated me in a way that is hard to put into words, the same way the love-in-action couple did. The two of them together reminded me of the night in *Clark's Diner* when they started playing that Damien Rice song, and these four people were giggling about something they saw at a Vietnamese restaurant involving a New Kids on the Block impersonation, and you said, "*that* is what friendship should look like—*that*," you said, "*that* is what love songs, romantic and otherwise, are about." It was something like that between these people with their respective eggs and toast.

I also kept watching these two people in a booth that could have easily held more people, despite the ability of these two folks to fill up the table with their own materials. It was kind of funny, I admit, to watch them. They were both working on something, who *knows* what, but I kind of had this idea that if you put a cigarette in the woman's mouth she would look something like an old-time reporter, journalist, whatever label, crunching on a typewriter in the 1920's. She could have fallen from the pages of a book, something like *Nevada*, or maybe *Sirens of Titan*, something less than mainstream and adored by millions, *I don't know*, and it was strange because the other one didn't look very femme, at least not at *that* point, but they both had feminine body language, and I imagined them fighting over who would get to be the wife with their matching wedding bands. I don't *know* why that was funny to me, but it was. It seemed like they were trying and failing to write at the same time, kind of like me, I *know—right?*—don't make fun of me, *okay?*—we all *know* you're the writer among us.

While I was watching the people, what looked like another couple came wandering into the restaurant. I know how you like to watch people so I'm just relaying the interesting ones, which (I know, *I know*) you've already figured out. Anyway, they were somehow mismatched and matched at the same time in both *appearance* and demeanor. The one with the blonde hair and glasses almost squealed at the thought of getting some of the sweet potato tots the diner now offers for some reason I can't figure out even though I bet your mouth is watering again right now, and the one with the long blondish-brownish-though-with-hints-of-auburn hair was talking about ways to figure out how many pancakes were the right amount. She settled on three, which she realized was a mistake right before I left. The tots were, however, not nearly so lucky. They were gone so fast that I almost forgot to mention them. I don't *know* why this couple caught my attention, there was just something about them that feels new and lasting.

Of course, there were more pairings and groups that caught my attention, but the only other one I really felt captivated by included two very feminine women, one who kept looking nervous and talking so fast and the other who kept looking self-conscious and barely spoke, who were reading together at another table. At some point (I guess they knew people there) they posed for one of those in-the-moment photos, and it wasn't until this photo that I noticed the connection between them, maybe emotional, maybe physical, maybe something else, but obvious when they focused on each other for a few minutes with their books on the table. There was *something* about that, something about the *disappearance* of the distance as their books hit the table and the camera lens became a companion, something about *that* spoke to me and to my ongoing curiosity about the different ways people relate to each other.

I also realize you're going to say that I was subconsciously thinking deeply about Alex because of their fascination with diners, and about *us* (you and me) as well as about Alex and me, since I only seemed to be captivated by the couples in the restaurant. You're probably right (you often are); I mean, I don't even know if any of the pairings were actually *couples* or couples-within-wider-relationships or -families, but *something* spoke to me and I would agree it was probably something deeper than one could put into the words in any given correspondence or communication. At the same time, I think I'll let *that* ruminate in the subconscious for a while, and just enjoy re-reading and thinking about the descriptions, like a historian mapping a magic past or a producer reviewing the ratings from the latest broadcast.

D ID YOU EVER TAKE A GOOD LOOK at the *Bear Creek* album cover when we had that record before we lost *so* many of those records moving around? I was looking at it in a store the other day and became transfixed for a minute or more. I remembered that it was the one of Brandi Carlile's albums that I liked the least at first, and that it took me a while to care about it. I remembered that it was one I accidentally got two copies of because I was being stupid and not keeping track of things, but that was *okay* because I think Mattie ended up with the other copy even though we didn't know them all that well yet. I remembered it was Tylor's favorite Brandi Carlile record, they said that not long after we met and not long after they found Carlile through some terrible novel they said they read to pass the time or for some reason I don't remember. I remember each of these things, but none of these things were what I was thinking about staring at the album cover. I know, *I know*, I always ramble my way to the point.

All those memories came back as I sat down to write, along with some others tied to that album, but what I was thinking about, standing in *Rock N Roll Heaven* looking at the cover was the ways the blues, greens, and browns of the forest on the cover blended. It gave me a sense of fluidity and stability, and it kept taking my mind back to that day I told you about when Alex and I were standing on the platform on the far side of the Gainesville I-75 rest stop looking out at Payne's Prairie. It was such a beautiful view. I can almost see it if I close my eyes. Alex was smiling, and the wind was popping against us and through the greens, browns, and blues below us that make up the seemingly endless prairie from that vantage point high above the rest stop. There was a sense of peace, maybe perfection or satisfaction or *something*, in that moment that I don't think I ever imagined finding in this life. We were just *standing* there, but at the same time, it felt like that view was meant for us.

I was probably thinking about these things because Alex called me that morning before I went over to Orange Avenue to absentmindedly look at records. They said they missed me, and they said to tell you *Hey*. I don't *know* how they know that you are here, but they always seem to know things there would be no way for anyone else to know. Maybe *you* told them. I still don't know if y'all ever talk, but I wonder about it. I still shudder (like at the first taste of a good meal) whenever they say they miss me. It surprises and thrills me. I don't know *how* or *why* they miss me. You said it was because they touch me in some kind of real way that you never can, but that is another one that you say I will understand *someday* when the time is right, even though I still don't quite get it in any logical sense. I say *"logical sense"* because you were right, *okay?*—I admit it, I have *felt* it emotionally for the whole time I've known them. I don't *know* what it is, and as you know, the best way I can describe it is that *something* in their eyes, or maybe it's their voice, *something* about them allows me to understand that U2 song you love called: "Sometimes You Can't Make It On Your Own."

Of course, even *that* song has more meaning for me since finding Alex all those seemingly-endless-but-actually-only-a-few years ago. They said, that song explains our relationship, (yours and mine) *that* song is why they say we've managed to cling to each other for our whole lives. They say we understood the need for unconditional love, for company at any good-and-bad point, for someone to understand and care and just *try*, no matter what—they say *that's* why we mean so much to each other, even after all we've seen. They say *you* are a part of *me*, and *I* am a part of *you*. They say *that's* what the song is about—that *you're* the reason I never forgot how to sing. Did you know they see us that way? I *know* you've always said they were special, that there was something about them that would make it the biggest regret of my life if I didn't become worthy of their attention, and willing to do *anything* to keep enjoying their powerful presence, as long as they would allow me to do so. I *know* you always knew many of the things I figured out more slowly, and I guess they often seem to have that gift.

I don't really know how either of you do it.

I also don't know how either of you have managed not to get tired of me yet. There are too many hurdles and falls between us to rehash all *that*, but I wonder about them. There was the time I abandoned them (you can put it in nicer words but we both *know* what I did), and yet somehow they let me beg and work my way back into their arms when I realized they were *something* and *someone* I could not run away from and remain whole. There was the time I felt like I utterly failed to help them enough when they went through their own issues and abandoned me as well. I did the best I could, but I couldn't do much. I just held on and waited, but I wanted to find a way to take all their pain away, and on that point, I always feel like I could have done more. *These,* of course (like the times we have spent apart), are only the big things, but the day-to-day ups and downs, runs and returns, *disappearances* and *reappearances* that are *me*—they (for reasons I cannot comprehend) seem to not only accept but even understand and welcome. You *know* this already, but I miss them even when we're apart for a second. I *do* think this trip to the origins (of me, *of us*) is important (*necessary* I would say), but I really *do* want to go home (as odd as it sounds to feel like I have a home)—I miss it, and them, and *everything* more these days.

You warned me about this, of course. I don't discount that. I *know* you saw this coming when you first saw them in that conference center, lighting the room in a different way than the rest of the people. You said, "there's something about them, something that might allow you to feel whole." You said it, just like that. I thought you were out of your damn mind. I thought you just had too many cocktails the night before or something equally wild. I just stared at you with my mouth open. You didn't even try to argue—*remember?* You just said, "Wait and see Millie, wait and see, they are the sledgehammer of emotions you need, I can just tell."

THERE WAS A GARTH BROOKS SONG **PLAYING** on the radio when I entered the gas station near the house I grew up in all those years ago. I remember we had a worn-out cassette of the album, and we would trade it back and forth because we were so deeply in love with so many of the songs. It made me think about Josie. It made me think about the things that stick with us, the things that become pieces of us long after they mean anything to anyone else or even our conscious minds. I was walking in the neighborhood later, and I passed Josie's old house. I was smiling, *thinking* about that old cassette. She had her own copy, she said, because she "needed to hear it too many times to even *consider* sharing" with us, like we did with so many cassettes at that time.

It was one of those moments you can't predict, but on some level (below the surface of things, beyond the waking spirit) you hope to see someday. I was humming "A New Way to Fly" and remembering Josie dancing in the dirt road over near the house singing it at the top of her lungs, when a group of kids (three that looked to be dressed like boys if you're curious) came bounding over the old wrought-iron fence that Mr. Reynolds kept up on the edge of his property (I *know* Mr. Reynolds passed away years ago, but I still think about it as *his* fence). They were flying (like we did so many times) and off they went across the road and into the woods. I'm not even sure if they saw me or cared at all if they did. They were laughing, and one threw a rock as they left the road and disappeared into the woods like we always did. I wondered if there were still animals on the property like Mr. Reynolds had. I wondered if they were up there playing with the animals, stealing berries, or both.

I smiled at all the stolen berries.

Josie said the fence was a metaphor. She didn't make that up, of course, she got it from what her dad said about that cassette—*remember?*—we were out on the porch at their place and Josie asked anyone-who-would-listen, why it was called *No Fences*, and her daddy said it was because most of the time, "fences keep just as much *in* as they keep *out,* and if you get locked into one of them things in your head," he said, "you might never find your way out, even though any *damn fool*—" (he loved saying "damn fool," and we would all giggle) "could just *figure out* a way out, *hell*—" he would say and spit his tobacco out just at that point, "you just *jump* the *damn-fool* thing, is what you do; that's what you gotta *do* in life sometimes Jojo." This would be the part where he tussled her hair, and she laughed, and you mouthed *damn fool,* and I laughed. He was always happy to tell us things about the world he learned "fixing them cars," but only so long as we never told Josie's mama that he cursed around us all the time. We accepted these terms.

I will never forget Josie singing, "The Thunder Rolls" (which we later learned was almost sold to Tanya Tucker, or something like that, but ultimately became such a hit for Josie's favorite singer Garth) the next afternoon as she soared over the fence at the edge of Mr. Reynolds' property. We were amazed. She was laughing when she hit the ground. "Come on you *damn fools*," she said, "no fences are going to keep us out or in; remember what daddy said." We both laughed, and the next thing I knew you were launching yourself over the fence and I was too. We spent the entire day and a few more after that exploring all of Mr. Reynolds' property, and of course, messing up our clothes with too many grass stains, dirt- and mud-generated, abstract, artistic pieces with a jeans background, and naturally all the stolen berries we could eat and smear on our faces. It became a mantra for Josie. "No fences you *damn fools*," she would say every time we were hesitant to try something, every time the fear got too real.

I was thinking about these things as I found myself in Blanchard Park later that night. I should have thought to check the park hours, but for some reason I didn't. I was walking back to where I parked and I came to a locked gate that had been open before dark. I could hear Josie in my head, it was like she was shouting from the next life, and I thought, *what the hell. That* was how my almost forty-year-old ass remembered to live as if there were no fences, and also how I tweaked my knee, (which you asked about this morning) by trying to fly again, realizing that, even with a little pain from a sore landing, some flights are worth the risk.

Maybe, I keep thinking today, *that*'s what this whole trip is, maybe I'm yet again learning some new or fresh or, *I don't know*, maybe just the *next* way to fly.

S O, I REALIZE I WAS JUST WRITING a few hours ago and I *know* I should be thinking (or "reflecting," as you like to say) on the idea I had about fences, but my tweaked knee today just reminded me of something and I wanted to share that with you. I don't *know* why, *okay?*—but sometimes I just feel like I have to transmit *everything* to you so that I can somehow make it all seem more real, which I know is especially ironic considering our relationship, but just deal with it. I love it how I try to sound tough, but as you say, "it never works." You always used to say I was more like a soft 1950's country song, rather than anything scary or loud, but what are you going to do—*right?* I also just realized that you would have had no way of knowing I didn't take a day or so before writing again—but there we have it again; I don't *know* how to hide anything from you anymore, if I ever did in the first place, so I guess that's just the way it goes.

Anyhow, the reason I picked up the pen again is because my knee is aching just a little bit, like it does sometimes on cold days, and that reminded me of the accident in 1996. I *know* you remember it, though we never talked about it much. I guess because I didn't want to talk about it at first, and then 1998 came and we just kind of had to shift everything about us and our lives and well, *everything* as a result. I was thinking about it though, I mean, what might my life have looked like if I hadn't fallen off that dirt bike at exactly the right time to mess up my knee, finish my athletic aspirations without ceremony, and spend all that time realizing just how privileged people who can walk are to be able to walk. I can't even imagine it. I still hate that dirt bike. I still have never gotten on another one, thank you very much, and I never plan to do so again. It was just a tiny little fat thing that messed up *so* much, just to feel cool. I wonder how many things I could say *that* about if I took a hard look at the years.

I *know* you will say it is a waste of my time, but I do wonder about it. Would I have kept playing? Would I have gone to college? Would 1998 even have happened? Don't worry, I'm not going to try to talk about *that,* but maybe I *will* try to *somewhere* because I think we need to at some point, and even Alex says the same. I *know* you disagree. I don't want to be an ass, but I think you might be wrong on this one, odd as that would be, so just keep an open mind while you read if you can, but don't worry, I'll warn you ahead of time if I start writing about *that,* I'll let you know just in case you want to skip it or whatever you do. (Do you read every word of these things, I wonder now, or do you pick and choose? I don't think I want to know, never mind.) I guess I'm saying, sometimes I wonder about the other paths we could have taken if one, or maybe two things would have gone another way. Do you think about *that?* I know you say this kind of thinking is a waste of time, but I still wonder if you do it too.

T HE WATER SEEMS *so* CALM IN THE early afternoon as I walk around the circle for the sixth time. I am kind of surprised to see this place. I just took a seat on the edge of the circle watching the waves. There are chairs everywhere, all around the circle it seems. I'm at *Center Lake Park,* which is apparently an amphitheater and cultural-center-type-thing they built in Oviedo at some point I can't seem to ascertain. There are children playing. There is a splash pad. There are couples of various ages walking around the circle together. You would especially like the chessboard tables on one side of the lake. There were two games in progress when I walked by. I could almost see you smiling over some brilliant move right before destroying me. I was just roaming around the town today because I wanted to *think.* I didn't know this was here, and I wasn't even all that sure where I was exactly, but then I stopped, picked a parking spot, and I've been here for about four hours now. It has a peaceful feeling I associate with other parks we have been to throughout the country over the years, and I *like* that feeling more than I can say.

Mattie called this morning. They're taking a break from their work and roaming around Ohio with their partner. There is apparently some kind of music festival or something going on at one of the liberal arts colleges in the state. Ohio is where their partner went to college. I think this relationship is more than good for them, and I'm kind of happy and amazed that they are going on a trip together. I hope it goes well, and I'm sure I'll hear more than I really want to about it when it comes to an end sometime next week. I was thinking about Mattie earlier today, so the call seemed to come at the perfect time. I was wondering how they were doing now that they're almost done with whatever-the-hell graduate program they are in; I still don't understand, no matter how many times Alex tries to explain it to me, but it seems interesting. I was wondering how they were doing, and then the phone rang just as I entered this park. I smiled as I heard their voice (in that way you say I always do) and I remembered when we used to walk over to that law school near the cheap apartments. We would sit at the stone tables, not unlike the one I'm at now, laughing and cutting up for hours. I never would have thought that was the beginning of such an important relationship, but I guess we never know.

Sometimes, I feel like *not-knowing* might be the heart of life. I *know* I've said this before, but I feel like our desire to pretend we really know what's going on—what's coming next and other things—is more like an expression of *fear* than an embrace of living. I often think that life itself happens to us no matter what we do or do not *know*. I think it just kind of flows like a river no matter what we might think or want or expect, and I guess I kind of *like* that, even at times like *this* when I'm trying to figure out something, like: how I can *know* what the *difference* is (or *means*) between the way *you miss me* and the way *I miss you*—or something along those lines.

I guess it's like Cole says sometimes, "I just have to dig

in, try my best, and see what the hell I can convince myself
I've figured out this time"—until the next time I realize I'm
completely clueless about damn-near everything. *That*, I guess,
is what I would say life *really* is (if it really is anything), but I'll
leave it at that "rant-over" as you might say.

GOT DRUNK LAST NIGHT. I KNOW THAT
is not something I do much anymore, but I did last night.
I was thinking about us. I was thinking about Josie. I was
thinking about Peter. I was trying to see something in them
that remained in me. I was trying to write Alex a letter about
everything I am feeling. I was writing in a peach-colored
notebook. I might have lost the notebook at some point. I might
find it later. It was the kind of notebook we used to trade back-
and-forth when we were kids. I got Mattie one too. They don't
know this yet, but they *like* writing in notebooks, so I thought
it was fitting. I guess these days *everything* is fitting to give to
you, Alex, and Mattie, even if no one else ever sees or hears
about it. I guess I could make *that* make sense.

I got drunk last night.

I made the mistake of reading some novel with a sad
ending written by some very likely "sad soul" who apparently
lives in Orlando (judging by their social media), who writes
sappy (though somewhat comical) works about the southeast
and people you might not expect to see in the southeast. Bex-
Something, who cares? their name doesn't matter. The ending
bothered me so much I threw the book against the wall. It was
one of those things where you *know* something bad is coming,
but you have to see what it is just in case it's something else.
The book made a quiet noise when it hit the wall. I grabbed
a scarf (the one you got me that looks like it could be out of a
Dawson's Creek scene) and started driving west just like it was
1998 again. I didn't make it all the way to Tampa, or even

Lakeland. Instead, I stopped at the pizza place with Josie's name on it. I got a calzone I barely ate. I heard someone who somehow sounded like Mattie talking about basketball, even though Mattie has never shown interest in basketball. I picked at the calzone, wrote in the notebook, and had the first of beer of the night.

I got drunk last night.

This is why the beer I had at the restaurant with Josie's name on it was only the first. I was wondering if Josie would like the place that carried her name back to me. I could see the face of fifteen-year-old me at the hospital that night. I could see the wreckage that was left of what was once the car Josie drove, the one that "even a *damn fool* could win a drag race with," her daddy said. I could see the people in the hallways of the small medical center (though we didn't know it was small at the time, there was still so much we didn't know, even *then*)—looking at us with a mixture of sympathy, fear, and caution. I could see the scraps of Josie's Pink Floyd t-shirt (the one with the **PIPER AT THE GATES** insignia on the sleeve, the one we never could find another one of, no matter how many Pink Floyd shirts we looked at in the coming years)—on the floor near the place where the ambulance parked. I wondered what the protocol was for those scraps. Was there someone whose job it was to pick them up at the appropriate time? Would they *always* be there—if only in our minds?

I got drunk last night.

I *know* this because: After the pizza place with Josie's name I already felt uncertain about my car. I waved at it for some reason as I walked to the *7-11* next door, picked up a pack of those cigarettes Margo used to like so much, and stared at a woman who reminded me of Cole on a bed (in that northern city, laughing at a tie-dye banner that felt like a memory that Cole never explained). It wasn't Cole, of course, Cole is in South Carolina playing with the foxes, probably pissed at Lewis (though we both *know* I see them *everywhere* these days). I smiled at the accent of the man ringing up my purchase and then walked in the opposite direction of where I'd left my car. I *know* I was still drunk, of course, because the word "walked" in the previous sentence is "generous," as you would say. I found myself in the parking lot next door, but it was good, a good mistake I mean; there was a bar there.

I got drunk last night.

I *know* this because of the ash tray in the corner of the shopping center, you know the kind, a concrete-and-sand kind of thing—so much sand—and I just kept staring at it for a while. I don't *know* how it got knocked over, but I wanted to know. Somebody was playing what I'm almost certain was the new Beck album from a burgundy car in the parking lot. I was listening. I could say that I was dancing along (to hide the swaying). I had a few more drinks (though the number escapes me) in this little hole-in-the-wall place (the kind we always loved) called *The Florida Taproom*. There was some long-haired, hippie-looking lady reading a book about Garth Brooks (of all people) and lots of people playing pool—and some football (the American kind) highlights playing on a bunch of televisions. I wondered what you would think of the place. Have you been there?

I got drunk last night.

I *know* this because my text messages this morning are full of sappy, failed, poetic thoughts that I don't remember having or sharing with anyone. But I did. I also asked *Mattie* about driving, for some reason that makes no sense this morning; I think I was thinking about Josie at that point, but I might have been hoping to have a designated driver if Mattie happened to be in Orlando or somewhere else next time I was drunk—*I don't know*. I kept *smelling* the sound of the hospital (the night we rushed there to just-miss the chance to say goodbye to Josie's physical form); did I ever tell you that I always liked the way you referred to bodies as "our physical form only"—you said it was a shell of what we were, and that as long as memories remained no one was really gone. I thought you said it to make me feel better about following you across the country, but that was then, *these* days I think you might have been right. Last night, as the classic rock blared through the building (or hole in the wall), I could almost *see* Josie dancing to Alice Cooper records, singing "Wish You Were Here," and jumping fences with her Garth Brooks cowboy hat, or screaming a line from that Hootie & the Blowfish album she loved, as childhood and "teen cool" collided in our small town in the early 1990s. She said there was something magical in the danger found in a sports car, and I wondered about what kind of magic allowed her to continue to show up in my life long after the sports car was left in pieces.

I got drunk last night. *That's* probably why I have nothing of worth to say today, or at least that's the excuse I'm going with. I am snug in my blanket on the couch (which is nicer than one would expect in a furnished temporary apartment) just writing whatever comes to mind because "sometimes that's what we do," that's what you said, *that's* why I'm not just staring at some Saturday morning cartoons. "Every word on the page," you always said, "is an attempt to connect, an attempt to remain alive in the midst of devastation, an effort to transmit ourselves to others (past and future), an attempt to be more than whatever we feel inside by giving someone else a small chance of finding some piece of us." I still don't know if I agree with that idea, but you said it (like so many things) *so* much better than I can think to improve it, and so I'll go with it now, let my head come back to me in its usual course—and miss you and Josie *so* much—scattered in scraps and pieces across highways and empty fields.

"NEVER THOUGHT I WOULD SEE YOU HERE again," she says, smiling and sitting across from me at a bar in Oviedo.

She calls me the name they tried to stick me with, a false label I left here in 1998. There is a piece of tape on the floor. It says "the bull starts here." I think it has something to do with the dart boards, but I'm not sure. She is dressed like something out of *Southern Living,* or a catalog for housewives and Bible-study ladies, and sipping what I'm willing to bet is a drink far stronger than its pink color might suggest. She is twirling her black hair with one finger and staring at me. I did not intend to run into anyone I would recognize from the past, but there you go, I guess that's always the trick when one arrives home again. For some reason, the song "Oh My Heart" by R.E.M. starts playing in my head, and I chuckle. She chuckles too. I don't *know* what she is chuckling about. I wonder if it was just a nervous reaction.

"I've *wondered* about you over the years," she says, as I continue to try to remember her name, "you just *disappeared* way back when, and no one seemed to know what happened to you." She spins a finger around the rim of her glass. She is smiling more than seems warranted by the words she is using. I'm not sure what she wants from me. She keeps looking me up and down as if she's trying to understand the difference in my *appearance* or *something else* that *changed* over the past two decades. I was thinking, when she said hello (and I started trying to remember why I recognized her cheeks) maybe that "hello" would be the end of it.

I don't *know* what to do in these types of situations, and you're not here tonight to guide me. *Alex* would know what to do. *You* would know what to do. *I* do not. I just say, "Well, it was time for me to see the world so *that's* kind of what I've been doing, going from place to place to see what there is to see." It sounds just cliché enough to end the subject, and I wonder if she will agree. Someone who looks like he works for *Gap* (or some other store in the mall) waves to us. I don't know who he is either.

"*So,*" she says, still smiling at me in a way that suddenly seems like what your mom would call flirting, "are you back here—*for good*, I mean."

I tell her that I'm just passing through.

She says something about her kids I didn't know she had. She says something about her ex-husband I didn't know she had. She says some more about "the old days," as she calls them, and I find myself humming a Bruce Springsteen song inside my head, still hoping the conversation will end itself. She doesn't mention *you*. This seems odd to me, even though she never knew about you. She doesn't mention Josie either. *This*, I guess, makes more sense, because we didn't leave right away after Josie did. We thought things would get better, or something like that, or maybe we were just tired. She asks about my mom, but then seems to know more about her than I would have been able to share. *Mom*, I learn, left for some place called Lake Worth, between here and Miami, a few years ago to chase some vague dream, and no one has heard from *her* either.

I try to feel like I want her to be doing well, but I can't muster the concern.

Maybe *that's* my problem in these kinds of meetings with strangers who don't like that they are necessarily strangers because they know one of the names you've worn at some point. Maybe I lack whatever ability other people have to muster enough concern to want to seem pleasant or *known* in some surface way. Maybe *that's* the issue. I see how she wants to feel some semblance of a connection, even though we don't have any reason to connect, but I can't seem to feel the same. I always wonder if this is a sign of a broader loneliness, like what I notice in the malls I guess, but I have no way of knowing and it would take more effort than I'm willing to offer to find out. You always said it was like I was kind of "checked out" from the rest of the world. I feel it in these moments, as much as I didn't like it when you said such things; I guess we don't always like to hear others note parts of us we don't look at all that often—parts we put away in some quiet corner like an old t-shirt that didn't fit anymore, whether or not it ever fit in the first place. I guess that's just another thing I'll have to figure out at some point.

"WHY ARE YOU DOING THIS NOW?" Mattie asked, when we finally caught up on the phone the other day. I was having ice cream and filling them in on my Florida adventures. They were cursing about the weather in Chicago and wondering when I might come visit again. I was telling them about roaming around all our old places. They were telling me about a novelist named Ella, who they had invited to talk to their classes. I was telling them about writing again for the first time in a while. They were saying it seemed odd, or out of nowhere. I told them I didn't *know*, it just felt right. They said it probably had to do with Alex and I getting closer and closer to each other, and even moving in together before I took this trip. I told them, that was what *you* thought too. They said it was probably good for me to figure things out with you as best I could. I told them I thought it was more like I needed to figure things out, "to keep moving forward with Alex the way *you* want me to, the way *Alex* wants me to, the way *I* want to, I admit."

I think part of the issue is that it's getting easier and easier to admit what I want. Even when it *is* something I still feel like I don't deserve; as you always say, "I'm getting better at going for it." Like with Alex, you have been right the whole time. They are something special, something different from the rest, like you always said *we* are, and it just keeps building, just as you thought it would. I think about you helping me make Alex recordings of songs, so they could hear me sing when they wanted to hear my voice and talking was too hard. I think about them starting random wrestling matches with me in that apartment on the south side of Atlanta when I was living next door to that Bonnie lady that fed all the cats, and Alex was driving in to see me when they could, like I would drive to see *them* when I could. I think about how funny they looked explaining the merits and downfalls of tautologies, and how fierce they became when that woman at the Better than Ezra concert wouldn't leave me alone. I think about the realization that there are now times where I feel like Alex and I, and even *we*, have as many or even more "heart-fluttering," as mom would say, "memories together" than just you and I had alone, despite it being much less time spent together (as a whole) that we've been in each other's lives. I keep coming back to the shock I felt (and still feel) that you and Alex always seem to understand each other, and how important you both are to one another, in ways that it takes me longer to figure out.

Mattie is similar for me, I guess, they were just as much a surprise, though in a *different* way. I always thought only you or Josie could ever be the best friend (or real love) in my orbit, and after Josie went on a separate adventure, I just figured I would need to get everything from *you* because I couldn't imagine caring like that again for another person—*remember?*—of course you do because you thought it was hilarious that I even told Mattie they were "barking up the wrong tree trying to get to know me." They didn't care. Like the other surprises (that came in the forms of Cole, Ellen, and Tylor) they just laughed at me, and kept coming around and listening. I still say you were right that Alex was the key, but the strangest thing to me, even now, is that for some reason I responded by wanting to talk to them, to *know* them, to be with them in special ways that are not the same as with you or Alex but are special and amazing in their own ways, while also making me better and somehow *more* with Alex and you.

I don't *know* why I'm saying all this tonight. I really don't. I guess, as you always said, "we all have our emo days," those times when we're deeply emotional, overly reflective, and when something special is happening, hard or easy or anywhere in between, that makes us very emotional, like a push-and-pull between possibilities and dreams and fears and desires, I guess it's something like that for me tonight. I heard you leave an hour or so ago. I wonder where you stay, or where you go, when you're not here. You've never told me. You say I wouldn't understand, and I believe you, but I still want to *know*. Josie always said that was my defining feature, I want to know *everything* no matter if I should or not. Ellen says this makes me fascinating. I'm not sure if she's *right*, but I can hope for that, I guess.

THE DAY FEELS, *I DON'T KNOW*, BEAUTIFUL—even all these years later. There was something magical about it. It was the kind of day where even being stuck in traffic would feel like a miracle, a gift, a chance to explode with emotion at the greatness of life. There was a raccoon playing in the field. I don't *know* why I noticed that then or remember it now. You always said I had a habit of focusing on the most mundane or odd details in moments where I'm overwhelmed by this or that emotion. Maybe *that* was it. I stared at the raccoon, then back into your eyes, then back to the raccoon, then back to your eyes. I don't *know* what you were thinking. I don't *know* if I was thinking at all. I don't know where the raccoon went next, but it wasn't there anymore at some point. The rock it was playing on (beside a sunken stump of what was once probably a pretty tree) was empty without it, the same way my body felt empty of all the doubt, worry, fear, nerves, and other essentials that seem to make up so much of the absolute anticipation we have for such moments. I stand in the same field today. I wonder if I'll see a raccoon.

I thought about that day almost as much before it happened as I have since it happened. There was the way Josie moved her fingers across the edge of her shorts when she was nervous.

There was the way your eyes smiled at the next cassette cover or Grisham novel. There was the way your voice became what I thought of as a haunted whisper when you were very emotional. There was the way Josie's eyes danced as if they were chasing a falling star. There was the way the tattered, hand-me-down Baltimore Orioles shirt draped against the small of Josie's back, just as she was telling me the latest amazing thing about Cal Ripken Jr. and his family. There was the way the soft highlights, natural and odd as they were, stood out in her brown hair as she shook it against a given burst of wind. I longed for all these things in the context of a deeper embrace and have cherished that embrace even unto this moment.

I thought of the forest creatures, the raccoon and whatever friends it may have had, as our witnesses, as hands removed the not-namebrand Jordan jersey from my torso. There was the secret in the softest parts of my spine as fingers created shudders and shivers running down my body and the smell of the grass mingled with the smell of lips. There was the moment the pants my mom said made me look dignified shook off dignity for a resting place in the grass nearby, almost reflecting the blush on Josie's cheeks. There was the slight whistling sound as fingers traced the line of my nerves, which I was only just learning to feel. I can still feel all these things, the same way I can even now see that the stump is much more weathered than it was.

I sit down in the spot where our bodies became one for the first time. Even so much older, there is something in this ground that is us, ours, as if it remembers as well as I do. It's almost like I feel the edges of the dirt cupping my body now, the way she cupped my hand as our lips tried to find every way to know one another. It is almost like the blades of grass are a welcoming massage, not unlike the feel of fingers sliding around, along, and between. It is almost like the whispering winds pulling through the trees call to me from all my bygone years, like sacred aspects of the people we would become that somehow spoke to the depths of everything we could have, whether we knew it or not. All these moments rush through my head staring at the stump, listening to the trees, dirtying a different outfit, and collecting grass stains twenty years after our day in the field.

THERE ARE NO BROKEN BOTTLES HERE NOW. There is no sign suggesting anyone is watching, even though no one ever was in the first place. There is no remaining sign of this site being used for loading and unloading, even though I *know* you would remember the signs as well as I do: There were broken boxes here and there. There was that box cutter that seemed out of place and yet perfectly positioned in the right spot. There was that vest, kind of "orange meets yellow in a sun-dampened kind of way," you said, sagging in its loneliness on the edge of the entryway. These things are gone. The decorations around the sight have changed, but everything else is the same. And when I say everything, I mean *everything*.

Yes, as you probably guessed already, I am crying, though of course now I cry in a more recognizable way, instead of the huffing and shaking that happened when I was younger, when tears would not come, when it was too much to feel anything. Just like in our field earlier today, I can feel you here. I can see us here. I keep coming back to the last time we were here. You were having what you called "the worst day." It was early 1998, and we didn't know it wasn't the worst day yet. We walked here because we often did that to hide from "terrible." We walked here because this was where we went to make sense of losing Josie, and to remember that day in the field when everything seemed to make sense for just a small segment of time before she was no longer able to visit the field with us. We walked here because no one ever came here—*remember?*—the other kids thought it was haunted because of the story the old folks at *Town House* would tell? We didn't believe those stories. I stand here now, and it feels like it really *is* haunted, but by us or the us we were.

I guess the newspaper article you read last decade was incorrect. They never did, at least not yet, take the tracks up. They still sit there. I can see the more adventurous me on my knees further down the platform. If I close my eyes, I can see the pieces of the broken bottles from the worst day before the worst days in 1998. I can see where you broke the last one. You were "so sad and angry and everything like that," you said, and I thought breaking something might help. You didn't know what I meant, but you trusted my instinct. I was thinking about breaking bottles in this very spot, tossing them as hard as I could into the abandoned railroad track, to process the pain from losing Josie. You didn't know if it would help. I didn't either, but I wanted to help. You went with me to get a six pack of sodas in the bottles, because the sounds of crashing cans were not as satisfying, I'd learned in my grief. You stood outside the store. You were fluctuating back and forth all day, pain plus anger plus sorrow becoming passion plus excitement plus hunger and then back again and then back again.

I bought the soda and we made our way down to the railroad tracks that no one went to for fear of old stories. Our fears were much more immediate in 1998. Your body was tight, rigid, like an "electrical storm pulverizing the fluidity in the cables," as your grandmother would say, even though we never learned what an actual electrical storm was like, I still think of it that way. You didn't know if it would help. I didn't either. You said it might be more fun with beer bottles. We tried that later, and it *was* even more fun, but that day, we were too young to get beer bottles in a manner as inconspicuous as one needs to be to break bottles in the name of grief. Remember when we did it with vodka bottles at that abandoned bus depot in Greenville, South Carolina?—and later with *Snapple* bottles at the truck stop in Greensboro, North Carolina in the middle of the night? Until recently, it seemed like we would never run out of times to feel grief roar out of us and into the crashing sounds of broken bottles.

You were hesitant with the first bottle. You kept asking me if this really helped me. You kept wondering if it was a good idea. I told you there was something powerful, something liberating about breaking things when I felt so broken. You said you didn't know about that. I said I didn't either, I just felt it. It was almost like I was able to elevate myself over the pain, reclaim the power to break from the feeling of being broken, and process everything I was feeling that was too strong, too scary, too real, I guess, for words. It was a way to transmit my pain to another place, something that I could control and see, something like that. You smiled at me, frowned at the first bottle, and let it fly. The crashing sound on the rocks around the tracks changed your face. You had a look like a murderer in the heat of the moment, like a lover in the embrace of a multilingual orgasm, like a musician buried in a solo that held the secrets to the world. You looked scary and powerful and beautiful. You started dropping tears—the other bottles flew alongside curse words from your pretty mouth so fast that it was only moments before I stood there watching you cradle yourself—almost all the way to the ground but not quite.

AFTER SPENDING THE DAY IN OVIEDO VISITING our spots, I wrote the previous two sections, notes, verses (what do you call the portions of an epic remembrance?)—I never thought to find that out in all our time together, but I guess there is probably a word for that. I bet Google knows. It's not important enough to me for me to find out, but there probably is a word for it. Anyway, I found my way back to this little wooden deck overlooking another one of the million people-made lakes that are scattered throughout Orlando. I'm sitting in one of those chairs you like with the wide arms made of some indiscernible material and a big blue cushion in the middle of it. I'm under one of those canopies that look like they can protect from the rain until Florida hands us enough rain to wonder if the entire ecological system is just laughing at us.

This deck is actually part of a housing complex or neighborhood on the west side of the city. I don't *know* why I keep coming out here. It's almost like I feel compelled to this area at the end of the day. It somehow feels like it's more me (the me I am now, whoever *that* is) than the rest of the city. I watch the multitude of different body types, skin colors, languages and the like, roam through this neighborhood, and wonder why the entire country can't look more like this. The vibrancy, the color, the variation, there is something magical within it that speaks to a part of me that never fit in anywhere, and especially in the too-many places in our nation where everyone seems to look, speak, and act about the same. I still find it odd that the first time I came out here I ended up on the side of the road crying about Josie. I guess that's the way it goes, like earlier today, I guess some places just pull things out of us, whether or not we want to let them out just yet. I guess that's one of the ways emotions work.

There's an event going on here tonight, but none of the residents seem to mind my visit. Hell, they are so varied they might not even know I don't live here too. There's a DJ playing and spinning inside, and he seems to know the audience or neighborhood because he has already gone back and forth between mainstream Hip Hop, Central American beat styles, Salsa music, some electronica you would probably hear in the clubs of today *and* the ones of our younger years (as electronica never seems to change all that much to my ears), and some Creole- and Haitian-type rhythmic dance music like we heard in New Orleans and Savannah. He's even playing some songs that sound like that remix album U2 did of all their hits, you remember the one?—with all the electronica and choir versions of the songs blended in from time to time, and I think I recognized (a few songs earlier) the samples of Kendrick Lamar. It's an interesting mix and there are children dancing and adults dancing and people of all ages laughing and chatting in the clubhouse and out here on the deck.

While I was writing, they also fed me. I guess maybe they're feeding *everyone* because no one asked if I was a resident. A nice lady with a Peruvian accent asked if I was hungry, and I said yes, and she pointed at the line forming inside the clubhouse. She told me to get some food if I wanted some, and I thought, *hell, why not?* The next thing I knew I was at a table of people from six different countries who became friends watching their kids play at the soccer field in the neighborhood. We were eating red beans and rice, some of us had pulled pork, and others had plantains, and others had both, and they were telling stories about the year, about their old homes, and about the hopes they had for their kids. There was something both simple and profound in the moment that struck me like a song on the radio you have to record and play 27 million times because it just makes you feel something more than anything else for a little while. I found myself sitting there, overwhelmed and grateful for the rapid-fire conversations in shifting languages and the privilege of seeing such emotion come out of nowhere, from strangers, over a meal that was so much like something your grandmother would have cooked that it just felt, well, *I don't know*, almost meant to be, like fate or something else like that.

T HERE WAS A CHILD RUNNING THROUGH OLD Navy today when I was returning a skirt Alex sent me that didn't fit right, even though it was the perfect type because somehow Alex always knows what I will like (the same way you always did). The kid was maybe about twelve or thirteen, and was kind of running and kind of dancing at the same time. It reminded me of the dance *you* used to do, you and Josie, that was kind of a mixture of the running man, the robot, disco, and break dancing (all blended into one because Josie said, "sometimes you have to just mix things up" and you said, "sometimes the boxes and forms just get in the way of expression")—the kid reminded me of *that* kind of freedom, and I thought about that day in Josie's basement when you two debuted the first version of what I would call "your mysterious dance."

I'm still not sure what, if any, label would have ever applied to that dance. I guess we were always running into those kinds of issues. I remember you two first did that dance the same day Josie and I "made out" for the first time, and you thought it was, what did you say?—"so cute and equally gross"—was that it? Yeah, *that's* how you explained it when you walked in on us. You *looked* at me, *remember?*—you were so dead pan, I remember thinking, *why is he so serious-looking right now? What is he doing?* and you were like, you *looked* at me—and you were like, "I'm not up for this kind of torture"—in this way-too-serious-for-the-moment face, and Josie giggled. And I was like, "I don't understand," and Josie was like, "shut up and kiss me" (all Mary-Chapin-Carpenter style) and you would always laugh and say, "cool."

Yeah, but the kid kind of reminded me of you two doing your dance. I remember I called it "mysterious" because you did it that first day, after we all had been laughing on the couch, you did it that *first* day when the U2 song, "Mysterious Ways," came on the radio, and I *remember* you said it was about *me* because I moved you "in *mysterious ways*" and I said it was about *you two* because you kept moving in such "beautifully strange ways," and Josie said it was about *us* because we moved this "mysterious ugly little town into paradise *by being together*" in the ways we found out how to be with one another. You two heard that song, and next came that mysterious kind of mixtape-style dance that I still can't explain, and then I laughed so damn hard, just like I did in the store today, because there was such freedom and beauty in that.

"**Y**OU HAVEN'T WORN A HAT IN SO long," you said, walking up to me across the patio in front of *Austin's Coffeehouse*, where I was reading earlier today. You were right. We both knew it. I haven't worn hats in a long time. I still apparently like the same kind I did back then, and I haven't worn one since *well, shit,* what was it?—my early twenties—I guess that's it. It might have even been the end of our teen years, the end of the 1990's maybe, I'm not sure, now that I think about it. "What made you get a hat?" you asked, "and why a baseball team you don't even care about, never did, and especially now that you don't even follow baseball anymore?

You knew the answer to this too, I think, you just wanted me to say it. I don't know why you do that, but you always have, as far as I can remember, you've *always* pushed me to express myself, no matter how much I want to hide in my little notebooks.

"Garnet always does look wonderful on you," you said smiling, and took the seat across from me at the wrought iron table outside *Austin's* where I'd set up earlier in the day to read a book called *Gilead*. You sat with me for a while. I answered your questions. You smiled. I told you about the book.

"I think you would enjoy it. It's written completely in letters like the epic ones we send each other, like *this* one I guess, and it traces the ways life can shift and change in the Midwest over the passage of decades. I've enjoyed it."

You didn't seem interested, but then again, you're always more interested in music than books. It was nice. My coffee got cold. The daylight started to fade, but I didn't even notice. There were people talking about gaming and hard drives and servers on the patio before you arrived, but I never saw them leave, even though they were gone by the time you headed out to (as you put it) "fetch a proper calzone, if this city happens to have one in stock somewhere." You were always so good at phrasing things; I guess that's a part of you I envy even now.

You said I was wearing a hat because I was "waking up, coming back to life," is how you put it, and I liked the image of waking up from a long dream or nightmare. You said it was about intimacy, about moving past what life should be, and diving into a life of *meaning* with *meaningful* others.

I didn't *know* if that was correct, per usual, but I liked the idea. I said that I was wearing a hat because I felt like I wanted one when I was last in the Atlanta airport, but I had to catch my flight. You said it wasn't that simple. I said, "it never is with you." You thought that was funny.

A woman with purple hair and a picture of Woody Woodpecker tattooed on her arm asked for your chair. I was glad you didn't give it to her. I would have. There never seems to be enough chairs on this patio. If the speakers on the inside stretched their sounds out here we could play that musical-chairs game they made us play in gym class on rainy days, when they weren't torturing us by making us learn how to square dance or do equally boring shit from some western movie.

I told you I got the hat while I was in Chicago before coming to Orlando. You said you guessed as much. You said you doubted I could find a White Sox hat in this color somewhere else. You were probably right. I said I got it because Mattie is now a fan of the White Sox. You, again, said it was more complicated than that. I told you I didn't think so. I'm not sure if I was being honest. I told you about Mattie, Ellen, and I walking in the loop during my visit. I told you about the hat store on State Street. I told you I still think about that Willa woman I met on State Street all those years ago.

"She was too funny," you said, and I smiled. That was how *I* described her, and you remembered. I love it when you

86

remember things about me even from the times we've been apart—I'm not sure why, but I do. I told you, "Ellen, Mattie, and I all got hats that night because I wanted one, but I didn't want to do it alone." You said, "nobody wants to wake up alone." I said, "you might be stretching that metaphor a bit." You said I was still realizing what was happening to me, and *that's* why I didn't understand how we *missed* each other in *different* ways now. I said, "you should just tell me." You said for the billionth time or so, that "it doesn't work that way." I scoffed because I *know* you hate it. You asked how the trip was going and I said I felt like it was good for me. I said, "I *hope* it isn't a waste of time." You said, I would "find out *someday*, but—" (and here I knew what you would say so I said it too) "you will have to *wait*."

T**HEY SAID, "THE GUY YOU SHOT IS** going **TO LIVE"**—the medic said it to Lacey as we sat on the curb on West 125th Street in the middle of the night. *Lacey* didn't mean to shoot anyone. That wasn't why we were here. *Lacey* didn't *want* to shoot anyone. That wasn't it either. *Lacey* didn't even own a gun. I learned that later in the day when she mentioned she had never even fired one before that night. Lacey and I didn't even know each other (to tell the truth in this moment) unlike what we told the medic and the cop that night. Lacey was just stepping outside her apartment. She was just taking in the nighttime air. She was in the wrong place at the wrong time. I was too. We were not acquainted, but the incident with the gun changed all that. Funny how a single moment can rearrange the connections, or lack there of, between people (or maybe not so funny). Lacey sat on the curb shaking. I was shaking too.

This may be one of the few things I never told you about yet, and I'm not sure why I am now.

I was walking in the neighborhood in search of a ghost. It was a guy. I think it was supposed to be a guy (but who *knows*) from a small town in Louisiana that was supposed to have some answers. At the time, all I allowed myself to remember and think about him was that he was called Ridder, and he was in love with music, men, and beauty (whether any of this was true, who *knows*) and I learned about him when that girl you were so sure looked like *me* sent me notes about him from the hidden recesses of her diary in the summer of 1996. But this was about eight years later, and I was looking for him. I was curious. I wondered why the girl told me about him, and where she *was*, and what she was doing *now*. I wondered why I wondered, but you were still off on your adventures (out west) at the time, and I needed something to do because I was kind of going crazy meeting a *new* enemy (hidden in the shape of a friend) named Cocaine (on the east coast).

The night before, I had slept in the dorm room of someone I don't remember now, who likely didn't remember *me* when they woke up to find me gone in the morning, or at least that's the way I like to think about it. I still don't know where the gun came from.

Lacey was humming in the night, the way you can do in cities because no one pays too much attention to anyone else a lot of the time. I was coming around the bend in the road, getting close to an address that proved to be useless, despite finding it in what seemed like a reasonable spot in the address book of a woman who had every reason to know more about this Ridder character than she was ever willing to tell me. You jotted down the address for me *(remember that day in the house with the koi ponds?)*—while I talked to her about magnolia trees and rocking chairs and some story I made up about loving Tuesday afternoons and iced tea. She was kind enough, but always seemed like she was "holding on for dear life to something she should have given up years ago," that's what you said *(I wasn't so sure)*. I was coming around the bend and almost bumped into Lacey at the same time the guy came running from between the buildings and slammed into both of us.

Lacey was a single woman who worked a couple of odd jobs while also trying to act. She'd *thought* about going to school. She'd *thought* about going out west. She'd *thought* about marriage and children. She said she did more *thinking* than *doing*. She said she wouldn't recommend it. She said, "to tell you true, I'm not sure what I'm going to do if I ever get past *thinking* and started *doing* things." I enjoyed her company that night on the curb. It was odd, but at the same time, somehow it fit into the oddities that made up the rest of my time in the north. We didn't plan to meet, of course, and so it was only natural that I never saw her again after that night. What seems strange, however, is that I still *think* about her and wonder if she ever started *doing* things or if maybe she still lives in the same neighborhood *thinking* about what she might do.

That night, of course, we didn't have time to think.

Too much happened at once.

There was the feeling of the guy crashing into us on the sidewalk. There were the sounds of the other guys, (four, maybe five, it was hard to tell) coming through the alley behind him. There were the sounds and smells of the sidewalk as the three of us collapsed. It was not the most ceremonious how-do-you-do, I admit. There were the sounds of sirens already coming. There was a movement and a loud clank as something that I later interpreted as "the gun" hit the ground. There was a curse word or three, but no one identified whose mouth uttered these. (It might have been mine, I guess.) There was the sound of the gunshot: *accidental, unexpected, premature,* I would think for some reason, and it was (to my utter shock— thinking back on it right now) *almost intimate the way the three of us spread against each other on the ground as the sound roared into the night, transforming the sound waves, transmitting DANGER to everyone within earshot.*

The next thing I remember was the medic telling us our newly met, cuddling-on-the-sidewalk friend was going to *live*—and the last thing I remember was shaking on the curb with Lacey.

I don't know why *that's* on my mind today, other than it may be something you didn't know about me yet. Or maybe you knew (even though I didn't tell you) the way you sometimes seem to do.

I **DON'T KNOW WHY I HAVE GUNS ON MY MIND TODAY.** Maybe it's because I live in America where there seems to be a new gunshot issue, story, or tragedy (whichever term people are using at the time) every single day. Maybe it's because I woke up thinking about that night when I knew someone named Lacey, over a decade ago. Maybe it's because the first song playing on my stereo this morning when I woke up was "The Bird Hunters" by the Turnpike Troubadours. (Remember we found copies of their albums in that tiny record store in Greenville, South Carolina last year?) Maybe it's because there was a gun fight on one of the highways here in Orlando last night. Maybe it's because I finally visited *Pulse,* that bar where the massive gun attack took place in 2016, and that was the first time I'd ever even *thought* about visiting home again—to think about the past. Maybe it's just like everything else, it just popped in my head and seems like it might somehow help me make sense of things.

I was walking the other day. I was in *Audubon Park* over by the *Kelly's Ice Cream Shop* I told you about. Sometimes I park there when it is hard to park in the other lots in the area. I was walking, and I found myself in the neighborhood behind the place. There was a yellow rose on the ground all alone. It looked so sad in the trampled grass, but it also looked like it knew what it was doing. (I know, *I know,* that was something Josie would say whenever she saw something beautiful that had been battered and looked out of place.) I always liked that kind of feeling.

So I was staring at the rose, and it got me thinking about the turkey shoot your uncle took us to when we were kids. (You remember all the men, and a few women, and crazy-ass Josie almost dancing around with their shotguns and bullets in the night?)You said it reminded you of some of the horror stories we read about in that *Southern History* book Mrs. Collins let us borrow.

Josie was too busy playing with her gun, and she wouldn't say much of anything the entire night. I remember the point was supposedly to win meat for cooking later, but that didn't seem to be the point. It was like a church service or that scientific conference we snuck into in Indianapolis when we stopped to visit your friend that just happened to leave town the moment she heard we were coming to visit. The Pacers' tickets were too expensive, and it was *so* cold, so we wound up in that hotel listening to people with letters after their names try to explain to each other why their numbers were as good or better than the other scientists' numbers. None of them seemed to notice the irony of talking about how people needed to help each other when they were in a luxury hotel and there were people pan handling out in the cold on the back side of the hotel.

I guess maybe science is more about saying what we *could do* than *actually doing* anything. Lacey would be proud, and the religious people would like themselves more, I feel like, if they just admitted *that* from time to time, but that's beside the point. It just seems like often rituals are about different things than what people swear they are about in the first place.

The turkey shoot was like that. It was common folk making fun of life and living at the same time. It was people who had no reason to shoot guns finding reasons to shoot guns. It was the opposite of peaceful, and yet, it seemed like it contained almost no real violence. I remember when it was my turn. I told your uncle that I'd never held a gun, and he said everyone needed to know how to defend themselves. I wondered how shooting a stationary target could so easily be equated to defending myself. I also wondered if it might be better if we just stopped shooting at things we didn't need to shoot at because then I would not need to learn to shoot a gun to be safe. I didn't bother asking him these things. I had a feeling his can of *Natural* (what he called *Natty Light*) would inhibit his ability to answer me in any serious manner. I shot the gun. I didn't like it. I didn't win any meat. He seemed happy. Josie won some meat, but she always liked shooting guns every chance she got. It was an odd night.

A LEX SAYS, "YOU KNOW YOU'VE FOUND A GOOD ALBUM** when it takes you longer to get through it than other albums take." I was thinking about this as I wrote them a long letter this morning.

I noticed that the cover art you were talking about when you stopped by this morning has been on top of my record player since I got to Orlando. I picked it up my first day in town. I picked it up at the *Park Avenue CDs* place I keep going to as much as I can. You liked the horse imagery on the cover. I like the title of the album, something about the phrase *A Long Way from Your Heart* somehow speaks to me as I write these words, revisit our past, and *think* about the future I want with Alex somewhere north west of where I sit now.

I know you want this future too, and I think that you'll be with us as we carve it out, like the images of the horses on this album, but I'm starting to agree with you, that this visit may be necessary for that to happen. I don't know how you *knew* that, like you know other things, but thank you.

I was thinking about one night when Alex was playing Turnpike Troubadours songs on their phone and we were getting ready for bed. I was watching them spin around in some kind of dance that was hypnotizing all the best parts of me. I was wondering how long I could possibly keep them in my life. I had been writing to you about something else earlier in the day. You said you were somewhere in Arkansas. You were spending time with some songwriters who were interested in Florida. Alex was singing along to the songs in that voice that you said would make anyone jealous and willing to live with it at the same time. I was laughing at the ways they move when they sing, and tracing the shadows between the movements so I could recall them at later points. They played that song I associate with Cole, the one about the Laurie character, about how (even deeply in love) things can go *so* wrong, and something inside me shook in a way that I still don't know if anyone other than Alex could ever cause.

I was watching them. They were laughing. There was something special in that moment that I have never found words to capture, even though *you* probably could make it poetic, since you and Alex both have that talent.

I was *thinking* about these things as I noticed that, despite spinning this record *so* many times in the past few months, I have yet to make it to the second vinyl in the set. I find so much joy and emotion in the first vinyl that the second one simply sat unnoticed for the most part while I played the first one so many times. I guess this album is *"so* good," Alex might say (Cole or Mattie might too) "that it can be amazing and beautiful even if I only listen to half of it at a time."

I wonder if there are parts of life that are that way. I wonder if some days, weeks, years, people, connections, or experiences can be *so* wonderful that they somehow allow you to lose sight or even feel good about the difficult or terrifying aspects of other times and places and people. It feels that way sometimes when I write you now, when I cuddle up with Alex, when I roam around this or that town or neighborhood with Mattie or Ellen or Tylor, or when I get into some debate about this or that topic with Cole. As silly as it sometimes sounds to me, I wonder if everything we went through back then was worth it, to be able to stand here now in a *different* kind of feeling, a form of transmission, a special place and time, for even just a little while.

AS YOU KNOW *SO* WELL, I'VE ALWAYS BEEN A LITTLE amazed and fascinated by stars (I can hear you laughing now). I know, *I know*, "a little" is something I often say when I really mean "a whole damn lot," as you put it, when I mean, what did you say?—"*so* much it hurts to even admit how much." Yeah—*I get that, okay?*—I deflect, it's what I do, there are worse habits. None of this, of course, is the point. The point is that I *like* stars and sometimes I re-realize this when I find myself in a spot where I can see them in an extra clear light. This happened earlier tonight when I decided I just had to have some ice cream. I was driving on the west side, so I parked in front of a *Cold Stone*, but while I was eating my (yes, you guessed it) "cheesecake-and-peanut-butter-for-the-world" (as Josie used to say) "ice cream," Mattie called out of the blue, talking about an upcoming trip they have planned to see their parents.

Of course, I've always preferred talking on the phone while walking (in no particular direction) or driving (in the same manner) with a headset, and as a result I decided to roam around for a while. I was walking down the main road at first, while Mattie told me all the fun things they expected to do with their family. It is always *so* fascinating to me (in a kind of sentimental-beauty-kind-of-way) that they are *so* close with their family (I wonder what *that* is like). I walked past the usual shops you see on so many city streets. There was the fast food, the donuts, the not-quite-Chinese food sold as Chinese food with an American twist, and all the others you would expect. There were laughing teenagers coming out of the *Applebee's* saying something about wings, and a couple old men holding hands outside the *Starbucks*. It was a nice evening, but after a while, I walked back off the main road. Maybe I was searching for another Cherry Street or something, *I don't know*, but I found myself on a road behind the main road.

There was less light on this road, less neon and less fluorescent as well, and I found myself walking beside one of the many human-made lakes in Orlando. I walked to the bridge that was the next road, well, the beginning of the next road. I wanted to walk over the bridge, both because it was nice to hear the water below and because it was in the direction of the ice cream shop where my car was parked at the time. I stood there on the small bridge (maybe a block or less in length, just enough to cover the width of the lake passage at that point) and stared up at the sky. The stars almost seemed to be dancing in the night. They were shining down on me, and something just felt *different*, right, in the world at that moment. Maybe it was because I was on the west side and these days in town every time I move west I feel closer to where Alex is, or maybe it was because of the wide-open sky with only five stars (we *know* how I feel about the number five. I hear you laughing behind me right now) in the sky staring down at me. I don't know what it was, but it seemed special, so I stood there listening to Mattie for about fifteen minutes instead of continuing to walk right away.

Mattie was talking about feeling especially free and nourished after finishing the painting you wanted so much. They are going to mail it whenever I can get them the best address. We'll talk about it next time you show up to say hello, as I think about your coming and going of late. They said it was something special to learn about your emotional connection to that song, and what they tried to do was create a picture of us and them together in the scene drawn from the lyrics of the song. They said the hardest part was getting the paint right. They said it had to be right. They learned this from a neighbor named Shonna, they said, but I'm not sure what they meant to tell you the truth. You'll probably understand. They sent me a picture of the painting, and I think it's amazing. The buildings are both symmetrical and each is distinct. I can also see these perfectly drawn images of us staring at each other in the foreground. I'm not sure how they managed that from the recording and lyric sheet of the Counting Crows "Perfect Blue Buildings" song you love so much, but I think you'll be blown away like I was by the stars in the sky that night, if not even more.

In fact, as Mattie spoke, and I thought about the painting, and I remembered getting drunk here on the west side, I think I finally understood what you meant about that song. You said it made you safe, and I didn't understand that. You said it was a *feeling.* Safety (as we know so well) is just an illusion, it's a faith that some people are privileged enough to believe in for longer periods of time than the rest of the people, but you said the song *"made* you *feel* safe."* I didn't understand that until I was standing on the bridge looking at the wide-open sky thinking about Alex singing "Wide Open Spaces" hundreds of times in a row, while listening to the comforting tones of Mattie's voice on the other end of the phone, and thinking about the effort it took them to make something special for you, even though you have barely even ever gotten to see each other. I realized that, like you, they *make* me *feel* safe. They do it in different ways, but somehow, they do it. My "other," as you call them, "intimate connections" do it in different ways too, and I think that's what you always meant about that song. I guess I didn't realize it, but I kind of get it now, and I guess if I can figure *that* one out, I can figure out the *"differences* in how we *miss* each other."

Y**OU KNOW BETTER THAN ANYBODY,** well, except maybe Alex and Mattie that is, but you do know how I *love* to *think* about songs endlessly. Today, I've been thinking about the U2 song "With or Without You." I know—*I know, right?*—talk about a throwback to our youth, but hear me out, or should I say read me out? *I don't know.* Anyway, I realized I was playing this song constantly on repeat earlier today, the same way you and Alex both do with songs you *love* and *love* and *love*. I smiled at the similarity because this is something that (as you have noted with your fake annoyance face) I don't really do unless there is some kind of underlying emotion coming to me or through me when the song plays. You would always want to know what it was, and so I am following our tradition of telling you what it is once I've figured it out.

So, today I was wondering why I kept playing "With or Without You" repeatedly. I was thinking about it and even using that journal you brought by earlier in the week. I was drawing shapes like I do and writing poetry no one would want to see (my usual) but in between I was working on why I was playing that song so much. I also noticed that I mentioned that song in the journal last week because I heard it (for the first time in so many years) in a bar that reminded me a lot of a bar I met Alex at in Tallahassee, *Fermentation Lounge* I think it was called, before coming south to Orlando. Anyway, I thought it interesting that the song caught my attention the other day, (or whenever that was) and now I was playing it on repeat. I think it has to do with coming home to our origins, writing you these letters, and making sense of how terrifying it is to think of a life without Alex in it. I think it's about *emotions*, maybe about *intimacy*, and maybe about loss and grief in some ways. *Hear me out, okay?* I know it is not a song you care for much, but I think, regardless of the song, that *this* part is important.

I don't know what the song means to other people (as usual, I've never bothered to look up what the band or the experts think, the way you often do) but I was thinking it was a good metaphor for trauma. The big hook is the realization that one cannot live *with* something that one also cannot live *without*, and this struck me as a true statement (however unintentional) about *trauma*. It is deeply hard to live without some kind of trauma, as we have learned from so many people, if you are going to be in any way *different* from expectations or *free* or *creative* in "the America of our lives," as we say. Damn near everyone we have met that is *different* from American norms in any way has experienced some form of *trauma* (at some point) that dramatically altered who they were, how they saw the world, and the ways they felt about themselves (for better, worse, or both) over the course of time. You *know* I'm right. You mentioned this too (at one point) in different words, and unrelated to this song (which I know you are not a fan of in the first place).

The thing is, I keep *wondering* (especially now that I'm visiting where we came from in such an explicit way) can people really live without trauma in the America of our lives? Think about it. If you are in any way *free* (so in any way *different* or creative or unexpected) you are going to experience *trauma* in some way. That is just how "conformist" (or whatever buzz word you want to call it) most of our nation has become, at least since our births at the beginning of the 1980s. Everyone knows the right clothes to wear, the right way to talk, the kind of family they expect, even the expectations of a family, the expectations of this or that sexuality or gender, based on the rules other people created. It is enough to suggest we've become a religious nation, like a theocracy, whether we noticed it or not. There are rules for everything, everywhere, and if you violate them at all, people will hurt you in some way. So, *think* about it then: if you cannot actually be *free* to make your own choices or live life your own way without facing *trauma*, and if without such freedom you are just another example of *conformity*, another cog in the machine, then, is it possible to really be alive in America today without *trauma*?

I know this sounds like some philosophical stuff you might hear in a classroom, but I think it's what a lot of art is about these days. Think about it. You have to   the rules of others from the moment you are born, *right*? Okay, so when do you figure out what you actually *want, like,* or *are?* Is the possibility of figuring out these things even transmitted to us in any real way, or do we only receive regular broadcasts of the rules we must follow? The answer, of course, is you only get such lessons whenever you deviate from whatever rules or script (or whatever you want to call it) that other people forced on you. Well, if you *do* this, you will likely experience marginalization and some forms of trauma. Since avoiding trauma requires avoiding being a person with thoughts, feelings, ideas, and beliefs of your own (that *you* have thought about, questioned, and tested out), no matter how ludicrous or silly—are the people around us who have lived without trauma even alive? Are they just, *I don't know*, "potential people" going through the motions until their bodies wear out? It sounds crazy, I admit, but I think it might also be kind of accurate, or at least close enough for amateur use.

Since the song is about a feeling or experience, it is never spelled out all that explicitly—so I'm guessing many people could read some feeling or experience into it—maybe *trauma* is one of the things it could be capturing. It seems to be one of the experiences deeply embedded in being alive or in the ability to live, whether we want it or not, and *that* is what the song focuses on throughout its choruses and refrains. Of course, if I may really annoy you by drawing this interpretation out as far as possible, you could then say the haggard screams in the song that Bono does are the screams of someone facing their trauma and beginning to retake their life. You could then say the angelic high notes held a few moments later represent the possibility of finding peace, freedom, maybe even an actual *life* following the trauma. I'm not saying I'm right, of course, but maybe consider it for a few minutes.

DON'T WRITE DRUNK. I READ THAT SOMEWHERE. I swear I did. Somebody said it. I *know* they did. It was that guy from that place that talked about that stuff we liked. You remember him?

Don't write drunk. I read that somewhere. I told you about it. You said what about Hemmingway? I said what about another beer? It was a Monday night if that matters.

Don't write drunk. I read that somewhere. I was laughing at you. You were drunk dialing people from the past for fun. You got their numbers from Google. You said it was something Vonnegut did. I asked if you read that somewhere. It was so cold. We were in that place, the one in Vermont, I think, was it a hotel or something? I don't know.

Don't write drunk. I read that somewhere. I took the advice just not to heart. You were giggling at the people you drunk dialed. I was giggling at you. There was a Shaggy song playing from somewhere I seem to remember a fireplace of some sort but maybe it was in a painting or on the television or something.

Don't write drunk. I read that somewhere. Why do I keep typing that? Do you know? Is it because I'm drunk right now? Is that why I shouldn't write drunk? Is that what the rest of what I read that said "don't write drunk" was talking about that time? I don't know. Do you know? Where are you tonight? I miss you but not the way you miss me lol. I'm funny when I'm drunk. Margo always said so.

Don't write drunk I read that somewhere I can't believe I typed it again. Maybe I should stop this. Maybe I shouldn't write anything. I don't know. You know what I do know? Yeah?—well, I know that something about a dark room full of people playing pool with the scent of cigarette smoke in the air and a banner like the one you had in that apartment you liked where you were so lonely all the time. . . . *Shit*, something, I was going to say *something* profound there. I really was but I guess I missed it. Maybe I need another drink but don't worry I won't write anymore or much more while I'm drunk.

YOU TOLD ME WE SOMETIMES TRICK
OURSELVES into not seeing something until we are
ready to see it. We were sitting on the curb beside that
diner in Queens (the one in New York, not the one in Georgia)
and you said that was the way the mind worked. You said it
was a way of allowing us to keep going and a way of balancing
the things we *did* need to worry about. You said it was a natural
thing, but that it could be jarring. You said there was no way to
prepare for it, but if you paid attention whenever you became
aware of what you were *not* seeing, you had a chance in those
moments to understand why *you*, or maybe your brain, would
hide things from you. You said this was useful to understand.

I remember the conversation so clearly. I remember the
sounds of the busses and cars on the road. I remember the little
Arab coffee shop where we got frozen yogurt because you didn't
eat ice cream and I didn't care enough to learn *why* at the time.
The guy near the window was reading a battered copy of *Fight
Club*. The woman outside was handing out coupons for free
soup at a new cart. You said you wouldn't eat soup from a cart.
Ice cream and coffee and pizza only, no other cart food allowed.
Was it a Tuesday? You were talking about the realization that
there were chunks from your life that you didn't remember at
all until we got to New York.

You were talking about how odd it was for those pieces to
flash into your mind out of nowhere like you were watching
alternative versions of reality only to realize that you were
finally accessing the things that happened that had been too
hard to face. It was like a secret radio transmission, you said,
like your own mind was faked out until you were ready to hear
the accurate broadcast, the real history, the part that wasn't
edited for mass consumption. You were talking about *trauma*,
we know this now, but you talked about it like it was a math
problem or a crossword puzzle, where only this or that piece
was revealed at a time. You said you felt episodic. You said this
ability to get away from the scary places in your mind allowed
your mind to finally show you why you were so afraid, but of

course, only a little bit at a time, because even tiny pieces of *what was* were far too overwhelming to see, no matter when they became clear.

There was the wrench that made your cheek burn. There was the closet in the utility shed you were put in for your own good. There was your mother saying *just be quiet and let it pass* and your anger at her refusal to make it stop. There was the blood on the sheets, and the smell of alcohol and aftershave mingling in the wind, that always seemed to make you feel dizzy in a bad way. There was the sight of the field in the night, the empty rows of nothing you ran to, when you were able to make it out the back door before it got too intense. There was the image of you, as small as you could be, between the appliances that were supposed to be repaired in the garage, hoping they would shield and hide you from the next tirade you heard brewing inside. There was the nagging suspicion, no matter how false, that if you could have just figured out the one right thing to do it would have never happened or at least stopped. There was the way he tried to hug you in the mornings that always felt both insulting and hopeful in a way that left you swearing there was something dirty about you that you could never quite clean. There was the indentation of a ring in your shoulder. There were so many sensations that went out of your conscious mind until he was gone, and you were far away.

You said this was the way the mind worked. You said you read about it in some books by a guy named Erich Fromm that you found in a tattered bookstore in a flea market stall in Augusta, Georgia. You said it was a form of self-protection, a form of survival, something like that, you said, something that didn't make sense while making perfect sense. It was one of those things, you said, and at times I realized I had my own sets of buried memories too. Mine didn't involve the same things as yours, but there were too many of them too. We wondered if those were the kinds of things that bonded people like us. We wondered if those were the kinds of things that kept our journey going from town to town. We wondered about a lot of those things, but recently, I've been thinking about another way we hide things from ourselves that seems both less extreme and equally fascinating. It has to do with that apartment I loved so much in Athens, Georgia for the four years I lived next door to that guy named Horatio who was fascinated with patios, adequate but not great Cuban food, and places named after military bases.

I think I was missing an important piece of information the entire time I lived there. I think it was there the whole time, but I think I hid it from myself, so I could enjoy what, you will surely recall, I referred to as *the nicest and happiest place I ever lived*. I remember that you were not surprised in the least that I only finally left that place when Alex wanted to live together. That was how I ended up leaving the best apartment, right there near where our dear love, R.E.M., and our later love, The Drive-by Truckers, formed. I left because living with Alex in Atlanta was even better, I just knew it, even ahead of time, just like you knew it long before I did it or Alex offered. As you know so well, I can't count all the I-told-you-so expressions you have thrown at me since. I love living with Alex and I love being in a bigger city, and with Alex I finally feel like I really have a home. I sit here visiting our origins, I think, as part of making sure I don't mess up what I have somehow lucked into up in Atlanta, and in an attempt to understand the concept of having and wanting a home in the first place.

At the same time, I am alone again for the most part, even as you come and go, like you always have, and even as I am surrounded by people every day on my jaunts throughout the city. This makes me think of the part of Athens (despite its magical qualities for me, after a lifetime of always wanting to run away) that I hid from myself. I was so lonely there. You once said that people can get used to anything no matter how good or bad. I think that was loneliness for me. I think about that American Aquarium song you loved, the one called

"Lonely Ain't Easy," you remember that one? I think about that song because I feel like the narrator; lonely was such a big part of my life (especially since we left here in 1998) that I think it became normal. Maybe it felt safer after Josie, after 1998. I don't know. I had *you* (even as you came and went) and I had *memories*, and I convinced myself that was enough. I think about the disparity between how many people I have met, touched, and known, and how few people I care for.

This seems especially salient to me now as I walk the streets of my origin city alone. It reminds me of walking the streets of Athens alone. It reminds me of living on a phone and in letters and in visits with Alex and Mattie and Cole and later with Ellen. It seemed perfectly natural to live there for so long (while feeling happier than ever) and yet at the same time, never making any deep, emotional connections with people in the city. I didn't even notice how much time I spent alone. I didn't even notice I *missed* something in the process. I must have hidden it from myself somehow, the same way we do with traumatic events, with the nightmares that we hope will go away. I didn't realize it until I had to be alone again. It's not the same as it was in Athens. It is not natural anymore for me. I flip through photos and I wonder what the people I care for would think about this-or-that place I visit on my rambles across the city. I send more text messages about this place. I send more small letters about that idea. I spent all that time in Athens happily, I thought, alone, but now I notice it, that they are not around.

I notice it all the time. I can't turn it off, maybe the same way they, especially Alex, had to turn it on for me to notice in the first place. I noticed it the other night when I reached for my phone to see if Alex wanted to grab dinner, because we do that sometimes now that I have a partner in the same city. I noticed it the other night when I started to text Tylor to see if they wanted to see a show that a sign I saw said was COMING SOON, because we do that now that I have a best friend living in the same city. I noticed it the other night when Mattie said I sounded *different* on the phone than I did in Atlanta, more like I did when I was in Athens, without as much to say, without any real updates on things happening in my life. I notice it every night I come back to this temporary home, and I don't get to go to bed with Alex at the end of the day. I can feel it, a loss, something missing, something I didn't notice before moving in with Alex.

It reminds me of the terror I experienced when we were in Savannah for that one year before I went to Athens. I remember it shook me more than I would have expected when Cole headed north, and I actually missed her. I remember that I would spend days roaming around and laughing with Mattie. We would sit in the concrete hallways of the nasty apartment complex we lived in as neighbors, talking about nothing that could have been everything, and even crying at a stone table, making jokes about Narnia. I would then spend the mornings and the nights with Alex, getting to know *them*, frightened by how much I wanted to *know* them. My life is more like that now. I remember when Alex needed to stay in Savannah to get their career situated, and Mattie needed to move to Chicago to do the same. I remember I went to Athens at the time because I needed to figure out what I wanted to do with my life, and because it would be near Atlanta where Alex hoped to land.

I feel like that year was a hint of what was to come or what could be. Now, I think about—or I guess I could say I *dream* or *fantasize* about—a day when Mattie is nearby again, while Alex and I continue to live together. The visits and communications with Cole mean even more than they did back then, but I also secretly wish *they* would be nearby again. I think about accidentally finding friends like Ellen and Tylor, and how easily I can see and hope for them (as strange as it seems to the version of me that just wanted to hide for so long) to become pieces of me, like Mattie and Cole have, as they integrate into the life Alex and I built in the center of the soul (or heart or whatever it is that I didn't think I had before these people all

somehow found me) the same way you said somebody would
. . . *someday* if I just kept going with you and left a little piece
of me open. I guess what I'm realizing is that being alone
was important for me, for *us* I think, but I don't think I'm
that Millie anymore. I think the Millie of today *wants* the
connections. And so, I'll keep working on it, making my way
back to these people that have somehow transformed me from
a mask into a full person.

"**I'M NOT LAZY," SHE SAYS, LAUGHING AT
THE FACES** her friend is making in the clothing store
nestled inside *The Magic Mall* on a Thursday, "I just don't
like *doing* anything." Her friend isn't buying it. She shakes her
snow cone at the not-lazy one, and says, "I think I may have to
teach you what folks *mean* when they say 'lazy'." I'm not sure if
their laughter is real or something done for the moment as the
two of them leave the clothing shop without buying anything.
The shop specializes (it even says so on a sign) in the kind of
tourist memorabilia that my mother loved so much when I was
a child. They have all the Disney characters, and all the ways
one can talk about loving a given city on a t-shirt, wrapped
against each other on the mesh wire that serves as the walls of
the store. I look at them, knowing I don't plan to buy.

I didn't plan to go there (I should tell you that, since you often
wonder why I go to this or that place), and this time there was
no real reason other than curiosity, I guess. I was stopping to
use a restroom, and on this part of Colonial, the best option
that I could see was the Lincoln dealership. There is also the
added bonus that the dealership in question has one of those
fancy coffee machines Margo always loved, and leather chairs
for when I might (like right now) want to pass as a person-of-
substance while tapping away on this laptop. Did I ever tell you

I always thought it said something odd about her worldview that your mother called rich people (and rich people *only*, we both noticed) "people-of-substance." It seemed strange that *substance* was more about *money* than the person, but I guess now, after a few decades watching Americans, it makes more sense than we would have suspected when we were children. Anyhow, I stopped at the dealership to relieve the pressure in my bladder, "my back teeth were floating," as your uncle would say, and I just parked in this store's lot because I didn't want to park in the **LIMITED** (read "easily noticed") **PARKING** available at the dealership. I was walking back from the bathroom to my car when I wondered what (if anything useful) I might find in the mall next door.

It reminded me of the strip-mall-type flea markets we went to in New Jersey and Savannah, Georgia and so many other places. I really enjoyed the ones outside of Chattanooga (for some reason I can't put words to at the moment, but I guess that's the way it goes sometimes). This place on Colonial was the same set up as all the others, and not for the billionth time only, I again wondered just how conformist our nation could be. Everything looks the same, people dress the same, even all the cool parts of the cities can be found in every other city (that may have been the biggest lesson I learned from all our travels: No matter where you go you will see the exact same things if you pay enough attention to what is going on or what is "set up" around you). It was depressing when I noticed it in the donut shop in Milwaukee that looked exactly like the donut shop in Mississippi, but now I find it rather intriguing. I read somewhere that so many Americans almost never leave where they are from, except to maybe visit the most touristy places in a well-known city or "hideaway," and I wonder if *that* is how they avoid noticing these things.

So, this place reminded me of all the others, and the set up was exactly what you would expect. The floors were a simple concrete, smooth like a bowling lane, and easy to clean with hoses (like we saw that guy in Michigan doing one afternoon when their *"Magic Mall"* closed—I don't remember the actual name of that one). The stores are basically cubby holes of a sort, partitioned spaces creating temporary rooms where one can store their items for sale. This one used wood and wire to separate each one (the same way that one in Las Vegas did) though I remember you preferred the cinder-block look we saw in San Antonio. This one also had all the old favorites we have seen in so many others. It had the baby clothes, the out-of-date tourist shirts, the phone accessories, the random music store (that only had music from one particular nationality that would not be found on the radio or in the local record stores most likely), and even the cute little candle shop. This, of course, is what they always have, and even the other two I found in Orlando (near the theme parks) have similar options, but I always wonder if there is some kind of master plan each of these places uses when setting itself up and picking which vendors will be welcome.

That's probably a silly thought, I know, *I know*, but I do wonder about it. Does it say something about the similarities of the people in our nation that these places, almost exactly alike, show up everywhere? Does it say something about our collective lack of creativity? Does it say something about a nation with many religious people who crave familiar structures? Does it even say anything at all?

I don't *know*, but I guess I'm thinking about it because I'm wondering about this trip, these observations, all this thinking and writing I'm doing. I know this is good for me—*I get that*—*You* say so, *Alex* says so—*I get that*, but am I really saying anything or am I just "spinning my wheels" as Josie would say. I really don't know, but I guess that's the kind of thing you wonder about when you're almost forty and considering the many ways your haphazard life changed over time. I left and am back at the dealership again. Does that even make any sense? I don't know. This leather chair may be far too comfortable for thinking, now that I think about it.

THERE IS SOMETHING SOOTHING ABOUT THE BLUES song playing in the background this evening. I can hear you mimicking the sounds of the (I'm guessing) Gibson guitar making the sweet licks across the edge of the rough-and-ragged voice singing about the hills of Mississippi. I don't think of hills (as you know) when I think of Mississippi. I think of the three nights we spent in Long Beach, Mississippi what seems like an eternity ago and yesterday at the same time. Do you remember that hotel? It was post-Katrina, standing all by itself staring into the gulf? Long Beach had nothing else except that *Waffle House* and that seafood restaurant. Remember we ate at both. We had that room with the too-ugly-for-words burgundy chair, and we would stare out into the gulf wondering what might be coming next.

I remember walking into the town and finding that coffeehouse that had once been a bank. You said you just had to write there. I said I wanted a muffin. You said the patio outside (which was really just an old concrete walkway between the bank and the building next door that the coffeehouse had put tables in) was ideal for writing. I said the muffin was better than I expected. You said you wondered why poetry wasn't as easy to write as wine was to drink. I said I missed the sign we had that said something about **WINE** and **POETRY IN A BOTTLE** that you got from that goofy women's wear shop in Valdosta, Georgia. You said the sign was misleading, but you smiled in a way that told me you missed it too. We were on that patio for two hours before you spoke again. You wondered what there was to do, and I wondered in return about maybe finding a bookstore or a slice of pizza. You said you heard someone mention a pizza place.

We were maybe two miles from the pizza place when we found the bookstore that was in a building we were both sure had once been a convenience store. We were walking, *remember?* because we only had enough gas to get up to Mobile where your friend from Nashville was supposed to meet us a couple days later. The always-kind-of-busted-up, gray, 1993 Oldsmobile we got from that lady in South Carolina just sat at the hotel those days. We both wondered if it would crank up again whenever we got ready to leave for Mobile. Your friend was coming down to do a show at one of the clubs in Mobile. It was fortuitous because he owed you like 400 bucks, but we had cut a deal because we needed cash, so he would have *200* on him in Mobile. I remember you met him at that *Best Western* in Memphis, but I don't remember more about him or why you were in Memphis. Maybe it was something about poetry, or maybe you just had too much wine and got lost again.

Remember when we used to ride the trains for the fun of it? They were cargo trains. We would catch them at the edge of this or that southern town. They had CSX painted on them. We even found some open cars. We would ride with them wherever they were going without a care in the world. Then, we would panic when the ride was over. We had to figure out how to get back to wherever we called home before hopping on the trains. We had to figure out a good excuse if we got back and had not already lost whatever jobs with whatever meager wages. We never seemed to remember to bring anything with us, but that was probably because we always thought to get on the trains after we had already had way too much to drink to be making any kind of decisions about anything. It was such a strange juxtaposition. One moment or day we would be waving to children playing near the train tracks who wondered (we imagined) why we were riding on the empty trains. Then the next moment or day, we were searching frantically to find a way back to where we had been before we got on the trains and waved at the children who were laughing at us on the trains. Sometimes I feel like, with the proper time and motivation of course, I could turn that into a metaphor of my life.

We spent three hours in the bookstore-that-might-have once-been-a-building for an entirely different purpose. We looked at everything they had, and we listened to that older woman talk about how much and how little had changed in

Long Beach since the hurricane. She was animated when she spoke, you said so. I wasn't sure what that meant. You said it was important for some reason you read about in some book years ago. You thought she might be suffering *grief.* I thought she was going to burn the place down because she seemed to forget her cigarette every few minutes and just set it down anywhere (in a shop entirely full of paper). You said she reminded you of a "dream deferred." I said she reminded me not to smoke in a room full of paper without an ashtray. You said I was being too critical. I reminded you that I wasn't the one who lost all our cash at the *Harrah's* in New Orleans. We walked back to the hotel that night in silence. You were thinking about the lady. I was doing my best imitation of a me-that-wasn't-sorely-pissed-off-at-you-for-losing-our-money.

THINK I WAS IN CLEVELAND WHEN I HEARD TOM PETTY DIED. I remember wondering if he got that last dance with Mary Jane, or if it was a pain that never went away after all. I remember watching people laughing over drinks similar to the one in my hand. I wondered if mine was broken. I wasn't laughing. Maybe I could figure out how they were doing it. Maybe not. I was thinking about this as Tom Petty began singing to me and the rest of the patrons in a bar called *Big Daddy's* around midnight tonight. There was something about the selection of "Southern Accents" as the song playing from the jukebox that spoke to me. Maybe it was because the song is not one of Petty's best-known songs, and I like things that are old, not as well known, but also not forgotten. Maybe it was because we thought of Petty as an example of a Florida kid who got the hell out of here and did well for himself. Maybe it was because the more-awful-than-usual karaoke was over and that made me reflective somehow. I don't *know,* but I found myself thinking about Tom Petty, and that day in the forest where we last saw that cassette copy of *Let Me Up (I've Had Enough)* that fell out of your pocket as we ran.

I *know* you don't like irony—*I get that.* I even appreciate that about you. I don't know if I've ever told you that, but it's true. I remember for a while there I thought (and you did too if you recall) that it was a dream I was having rather than a memory. We were wrong. It was a memory. The woods felt darker in the dream and that makes sense in hindsight, but I also find it funny that of all the cassettes you could have been carrying when we were running from those assholes that day, it had to be one with that title. I know, *I know,* you hate that kind of thing, but it *is* kind of fascinating to me.

I mean, the day started off normal. We went out in the woods. We sat by the stream, talking about music and school and other shit we talked about. We were just having fun until we heard the pellets cut through the leaves. We thought we were imagining things, and then we saw the splash in the water and the next pellet caught you in the back. You jumped. I remember that. We were scared. I remember that.

We started running through the forest in the opposite direction of the pellets. We thought maybe it was over because the sound of our footsteps drowned out the sounds of the pellet gun. We thought this until I caught one in the back of my calf. It was the right calf, I remember that. I remember we were surprised it hurt as much as it did. We saw Josie playing with her air gun a few days later, and we wanted to yell at her for no reason. It was such an odd thing. It was like our fear got transmitted to her in some metaphorical way too complex for kids to understand. In the woods, though, we had no clue who was shooting at us, and we never did learn or figure it out. I remember we kept running as fast we could, but they kept up for a long time. It seemed like time didn't make any sense as we moved through the trees, kind of the way time disappears during especially intimate moments, but not the same.

I remember we just kind of stared at the trees, standing

still for a couple seconds, when we got out onto the road. We waited. We wondered if there was more to come. There wasn't. We knew they wouldn't try it with cars and adults nearby, of course, but we still worried there was more to come. I guess I thought of that because that's how I feel right now. I *know* I need to embrace this life I have now, but I keep wondering if more bad stuff is coming. Can you tell me how to stop that? Can you look me in the eye like you did in the road that day? I think that would help; I really do.

T HERE WAS THIS PLACE OUTSIDE OF APOPKA the other day, advertising **ALL THE GUNS AND PANTIES YOU WILL EVER NEED**, and there was something about that sign that made me laugh.

After all our travels, I feel like I should be immune to the things you see in small, rural towns outside of cities, but some things still crack me up. My favorite remains the place that promised **THE BEST HAND-CRAFTED BUTTERFLY BERETTA'S IN THE WORLD**. I mean, come on, who needs a handgun in the shape of a butterfly, who is the target market for that? I know, *I know*, you told me then and you want to say it now, it means Beretta's with butterfly art on them, but even so, who the hell is driving in the middle of nowhere, in rural Missouri, looking for this product. That is what I want to know. I also love the places with the specials on **ALL THE GUNS AND AMMUNITION YOU NEED** that are right across the highway or street (or whatever it's called in the middle of nowhere) from the churches with the **JESUS IS LOVE** signs. I know, *I know*, I just love these things.

I guess there are things about the odd combinations people come up with that just fascinate me in ways I've never been able to accurately express to you. It just seems odd to me that *anything* in our nation can become an accessory for a gun. I feel like somewhere in writing we should just say that guns are the national pastime, but I know that the constant deaths that come from the use of these things make that tricky from what that marketing person we met would call an optical standpoint. The optics are tricky, he kept saying about everything we asked.

It just seems odd that a country so obsessed with talking about love, family, and all that jazz would be more than a little addicted to guns everywhere, in every way, and always. It seems almost like a type of bipolar stance, if you think about it. Or maybe we just *talk* about all the emotional stuff and love stuff to hide the fact that we all just want to shoot things. I don't know, but once again, I'm driving around out in the woods today wondering about stuff.

I decided to take a drive because my head was getting "too full," as your mom liked to say, "with all this reflecting stuff." Don't get me wrong, I still think you're right that I need to know why we *miss each other in different ways* now. I also still think Alex is right that visiting here, thinking about you and me, and reflecting on my life is important—*I get that*. I really do. I was a mess for most of my life, and now I don't know what to do with all this damn peace. I understand that I need to figure it out.

I think part of the problem is that I never planned to find any peace after 1998, if I ever did before then, but now I have that and don't know what to do with it. All I really know how to do is keep on running. All I really *know* how to do is communicate with you and keep damn near everyone else at arm's length, or maybe "two-by-four length" as you once said. I don't know what to do with stupid happiness or peace or any of that crap I had to convince myself I would never have. I just don't know what to do, *that's t*he problem, I *see* that.

YOU KNOW THAT WILCO SONG YOU LOVE
that I hate so much? You *know* the one I'm talking about because it's like the only song of theirs I don't treat like a Holy Bible of sorts. You know the one, "Country Disappeared" —yeah, *that* one. It was playing on repeat somehow (maybe the barista was in love with it or just torturing me, I don't *know*) at a coffee shop I stopped at in the Disney area of the city the other day. As much I wanted to ignore it, I could not. I started thinking about it, about the lyrics. How does Tweedy come up with that stuff?—you would always say (even after you read *The Wilco Book*), but I don't care. I started thinking about the song, and the idea of things that once meant everything but now are not the *same*.

It got me thinking about us, and I admit, at first, I was sad about that. (I wonder if that's what you mean about the different ways we miss each other.) There was a time when it was just us against the world, we were everything the other had, the rest had been torn asunder in the most brutal of ways. I wasn't Millie yet, or at least not like I am now, I don't think, and you were just there, like always, and I leaned so heavily on you. I think I needed you more then than I have in the last couple years since spending so much time in those Georgia cities, as you call them, that were more like baseball dreams when I was a kid. But I don't think it's the cities, if I think about it, I think it's the people. I think it's the connections I have made with loving people, maybe even the realization that loving people exist for someone like me, maybe that's it.

I was sad about it at first, the thought that you are not everything, or the only thing, anymore. Maybe that's what you mean. I don't know, but I was thinking about it because that damn song would not stop playing. I remember wondering if I could break the stereo. It is such a good album (well duh, you would say, it's a Wilco album) but that damn song. Anyway, I kept *listening* and kept *thinking*. I couldn't help it, and the sadness became something else. Maybe nostalgia. Maybe acceptance. I don't know what it was. I began to wonder if the sadness was just a gut reaction, a response that didn't necessarily fit anymore, something comfortable to help me *feel* or *think,* or whatever this transmission of thoughts is about, I don't know.

But I realized that it is *okay.* It is *okay* that you are *different* for me now, and that I am *different* for you, I guess, or maybe just different. It *is* okay. We clung to each other in the way you do when you have nothing else to hold on a cold night, but now that I have others who feel worthwhile (even though I agree with your thoughts the other night, that *is* a terrible way to explain it. What did you say? "Sometimes language cannot capture magic" or something like that?) anyhow, now that I have others who connect to me in positive ways, maybe you and I are not the same anymore. Maybe I don't miss you or need you in the same ways I did before, and that is okay, I think, and maybe that is good enough.

THERE IS A CHILD PLAYING SOCCER. The child looks like what we might call a boy. He is running in the soccer field kicking the ball with all his might. He is with two other children. His skin is dark as night. One of the children with him is smaller and looks like we might call them a girl. She has lighter skin of a brown hint and tone. She is following and kicking the ball sometimes as well. The other child on the soccer field is even smaller. This child is dressed as a boy too, but he has much lighter skin that people in our country would call white. The three of them speak to each other in mixtures of languages. I can pick out some words, and others are unfamiliar. They have found a way to "speak between," I guess you would say. They are kicking the ball, running on the field, and laughing between bursts of words.

When I got back from the coffee shop, you were sitting on the couch in my new hotel room. I moved here because the lease on my temporary apartment in Winter Park ran out, and I don't know how much longer I will be in town. You were sitting on the couch, and you asked me what I thought about when I thought about the home I share with Alex in Atlanta. You asked what it was like there, from my perspective, you asked what it felt like. I talked about Alex dancing to Spanish music in the bathroom. I talked about the shelves they made for my records. I talked about the art everywhere, and a feeling I can only guess is what people call home. I talked about the spot where I write in the mornings, and how Alex set up the spot, so I would feel at home when I got there from my old apartment. I told you about staying still and quiet in bed every morning when I first wake up because I'm not sure if I'm really awake or simply dreaming about the life I share with Alex in the neighborhood where I always think about the kids playing soccer on so many days as I walk past them to check the mail or stretch my legs.

You asked why I mentioned the kids playing soccer. You said it seemed like an interesting detail. I told you there was something about that image and the many more like it in the neighborhood that made me hopeful. You wanted to know what I meant. I thought about laughing and saying you'll figure it out when you're ready, but we know that is your line. I said I didn't know how to explain it. There was something about it, something that captured how much I enjoy walking through the neighborhood, hearing so many different voices and languages in harmony, seeing so many different skin tones playing and talking to each other in a kind way, seeing so many people of various types of dress or gender presentation or whatever you said Mattie calls such things, it just feels better than the constant groups of people that seem to all look, dress, and act alike in most of the country. It gave me hope for something better we could be if we all just embraced our differences and found a way to come together, maybe on a soccer field or in between the buildings of a neighborhood in a city.

You said it was my subconscious. I didn't understand. This time you were kind enough to explain. You said I felt peaceful there because Alex loved me no matter how different I was from other people, and that the differences in all the other people, the "diversity," as you called it, in the neighborhood symbolized these feelings for me. I'm not sure if I really understand that idea at all, but I like it. I'm not sure what it means, but I do feel safer with Alex than I feel anywhere else, and I feel like that is something special. Remember you said that you thought Alex was one of the few examples of people that could make me understand what it would be like to be "willing to go half a world away in search of love," I think I've begun to understand what you meant. I can't put it into words so nicely, but I think I get that now. I think you were right. I think I would follow them anywhere if they wanted me to come along, and I guess that's kind of what you meant, or maybe you were just referencing that one R.E.M. song that I love that you do not love for some damn reason that will never make sense.

THAT DAMN SINGLE WILCO SONG I CANNOT seem to love like the rest also felt appropriate as I sat in the coffee shop by myself trying to figure out how I feel about you, about us, about Alex and the others, and well, I guess, about me. I don't mean anything bad about my feelings here. No, it was actually kind of cute and fun because I was listening to that song on repeat and thinking about us and then Tylor and I had one of those disagreements you find so damn entertaining. They called me up while I was at the coffee shop. They're in Atlanta, finished with vacation and headed back to work, and they saw that I posted a picture of myself in the coffee shop wearing one of my band shirts that they like, and have a matching copy of that I left with them one night.

They were walking in *Criminal Records* (they had to rub that in, you *know* they just had to, it's how they are) and they were having an argument with someone else (I don't know or care who and they probably don't either) about the significance of band t-shirts. You know how they are, their rant-overs and all that la la la, but that wasn't the fun part. The fun part was that they noted that I left another shirt of mine with them, which makes sense considering they look so nice in them (and I'm *me*, I know, *I know*). Mattie still has some hoodies of mine from when we lived next door to each other in Savannah, but they were sure they already had a copy of that shirt and wondered how I got two. I pointed out that I actually did have two of that shirt, but they only had the one I had just left with them. They disagreed with all their might. It was like they were certain about it, which only made it even more hilarious that I knew they were wrong. They were mixing up two different shirts (and in this case, I *knew* that's what they were doing because the other one of mine they have from the same band is a rarity that is hard to find) that I gave to them as my own symbolic way of allowing myself to admit they are important to me.

So anyway, I know you like these stories, but it was even better, even before they realized I was right later that night and kind of admitted it (while kind of not) in text messages, but it was even better because it reminded me of when you and Josie got in that argument about the Pat Benatar t-shirt when we were kids. Josie was sure it had the purple lettering—*remember?*—and you were sure it was pink. You kept going back and forth so many times, and you were both getting *so* angry. Tylor was so sure they were right like you two were *so* sure you were right, and in both cases, you were all wrong. Josie—*remember?*—later noted that the lettering was a kind of red, but the one on the album cover you loved was pink and the one on the album cover she loved more (and even "*most* more," she said) was purple. I don't know why I'm telling you this, but it just struck me as *too* funny and cute not to share with you.

KNOW I'M DOING THAT OBSESSING

THING you always say I do, but I keep thinking about that day at the coffee shop and about that damn song.

I was driving this morning. I was listening to that R.E.M. greatest hits collection you found, *you know?* the part-this-and-part-that-and-all-that-jazz record they released at the end of their career. I was sitting in the car later in the day, and I just found myself staring at the dates, *you know?* at the end of the title it has the dates of the band, like something you would see on a tombstone? Well, I was thinking about that. I was thinking about that and that "country disappeared" song, and I wondered if that sums up my life to date. I know, *I know,* I'm obsessing, but bear with me.

I was thinking about my life in the midst of one of those tombstone dashes. I was thinking about that guy named Dylan we met in Atlanta, and the way he talked about the years as a dash between where we were and where we go. I was thinking about a book talk I went to here in Orlando where Jackson Garner was explaining the idea behind his latest novel and how he sought to capture the way the past feeds the present. I was thinking about Josie sitting around her house for hours that summer she was obsessed with Leonard Cohen records because she believed they would teach her how to write in a special way. I was thinking about that person we met who just went by "Kid" in Atlanta. I was thinking about that woman, what was her name?—Kelly, I think that was it—we met in Chicago at the *Cheesecake Factory*; remember she seemed to just want to drink herself out of existence as fast as she possibly could? I was thinking about what constitutes a life, and what makes a life make sense.

I was thinking about what my dash would look like, and I realized that I feel like I have two dashes in some ways. I have the days before Savannah, and then I have the dash since Savannah. Basically, I have the dash that hides what I survived to get to Savannah and find, I guess, my people, and then I have the time since where I've felt more alive, more whole I guess, even when it's been way too painful or raw for a moment or day or twenty. I was thinking that if I had to name the dash that starts when I got to Savannah, I would call it something like "Oh My Heart" or *maybe* "The One I Love," I told you I was listening to that R.E.M. record so don't laugh too hard at my obsession if you can help it. But at the same time, I was thinking about the dash that would carry me from 1980 until I got to Savannah, and that damn "Country Disappeared" song kept running through my head as the only proper title, though if we were keeping the R.E.M. theme going, I guess I could call it "Leaving New York" or maybe, if I feel really artsy, something like "Bad Day" or "All the way to Reno."

But I think "Country Disappeared" fits rather well, I mean, because that is basically what happened for the first 27 years of my life, if you think about it. Every time the next horrible thing happened, it was like another part of who I was or could be disappeared. I don't know if it was taken away or if I hid it *or maybe* you hid it for me, *I don't know.* At the same time, look at what we did together when it all got too much in 1998. We disappeared into the country, into the backroads and interstates of America, traveling across the nation. We were making sure no one ever knew us well enough for the pain to reappear in our daytimes no matter how much it haunted our nights. I remember reading a handful of novels in my twenties that compared people to places like islands, bus stops, nations, and other things. If I was a country, I somehow vanished in that dash even though I don't think I knew that until I got to Savannah and started to, how did you put it, wake up. It was like I became my own (I *know* you're going to laugh but I like this theme now so deal with it)—it was like I became my own "World Leader Pretend," and my time in Savannah, Athens, and now Atlanta has been my own decision making about taking down all the barriers or walls or whatever I erected in the first place. What do you think? Is that possible, or am I just killing time obsessing over the past?

COLE, I THOUGHT, *AS A WOMAN,* **WALKED BY ME**—too fast for me to get a good look at her. It wasn't Cole. Cole is in South Carolina. I know that intellectually. We talked on that new messenger program a few nights ago, and she is doing well. It wasn't Cole, but the lady looked so much like Cole for just a second that I stared after her as she turned the corner. Isn't it funny how that happens? You can see someone you have never known, and their similarity to someone important can generate so many emotions it becomes hard to breathe, think, or really do anything sensible. Cole would say that's because I have a "sappy side that takes up most of my other sides" when it's able, and Alex would say it's because my "hard shell is filled with a gooey core of emo fascination." You would say I just look for meaning everywhere.

Seeing the not-Cole lady who reminded me of Cole got me thinking about my daily life. As you have noted so many times, I really, on some level, have Cole to think for the lifestyle I live these days, and even the fact that I can come down to Orlando randomly for a month or so, and can do my work from anywhere, even this smelly hotel table that apparently was the site of someone's recognition that they had too much to drink last night. (I could move to another table, but each morning I've been here at this hotel, I've used this one, so I figure that is best when I'm on a deadline.) I have to finish that essay about the Old Crow Medicine show, covering that old Bob Dylan record Josie loved so much. *Okay,* I loved it too, so did you, and so did millions of others, but Josie was obsessed with the thing. *Remember?* she said it was "maybe the most perfect form of perfection ever perfected by a perfect person in the world." I remember you giggled and asked her if there was "room for another form of *perfect* in that sentence."

I guess in some ways I resemble Cole (well, the real Cole rather than the smooth, sweet-talking, smartass, former-beauty-queen Cole the rest of the world sees) more than even the lady I saw today. I'm sitting here pounding away on my laptop like Cole did while blogging every day those months we spent together in the sun and trauma of our shared (though diminishing) youth. I have a cigarette hanging out my mouth because I still smoke when I write because that was what Cole always did. *Remember?*—you said she looked like one of those journalists in the old movies. I write in these old, beat up, t-shirts like Cole did back then because, as she said so many times, "sometimes you have to feel ragged to create something worthwhile." I always thought that statement was equally about both writing and life, but Cole would just smile and wink at me when I said that. You said that was her way of saying I would understand when the time was right, and I said you were both smartass pains in my own ass.

As I submit the essay about the Old Crow Medicine show I liked more than I expected, I think about the genius of Cole's occupational lessons shared with me over too many glasses of way-too-cheap champagne in that ugly green bottle we got from the grocery store.

"You could just do what *I* do," she said one morning twirling her hair as the sunlight spread across her bare stomach. Her pelvic mound was quivering the way it did sometimes when we felt more affectionate in the morning, and I said, "I don't know anything about jobs." She was writing blogs about jobs while working on novels that were far more brilliant than I ever managed. I never understood her talent for words, the same way I never understood your own shared talent for the same. You two have this amazing way of phrasing that still makes my own clumsy, "oh-so-terrible" (as I always say) writing seem like it comes from a different world than wherever you two got your own abilities. "You wouldn't write about *jobs*, silly," she said giggling and rubbing the right side of her stomach, the way she did when she realized she was hungry before figuring it out consciously. "What would I do then?" I asked in my usual completely ignorant state, and she just laughed even harder and threw her pillow at my head.

I remember we were sitting outside the apartment we had

just moved into in Savannah. This was before we met Mattie. This was before Alex even moved to the city. We were counting our money to see how many days we could eat that week. She was worried about a course assignment for her degree. I was worried about annoyances at my job. We were counting our books and CDs, wondering which of the few remaining ones we could do without if we needed to pick up some cash during the week. She was holding a flyer for a place that bought clothes. You were over at the *24-Hour Coffee Shop* down the road doing whatever you did there all the time, probably "writing and dreaming," *right*?—isn't that what you always say? It was later the same day. She turned to me and said, "You should write about music and proofread books." I stared at her, and said, "I don't have any training that I know of for either of those things." Punching me in the arm the way she always did, she said, "You read constantly and can't shut up about music, you'll be fine." I asked how I would get paid for that. She said she knew some sites where I could start generating content, and maybe from there it could become a job.

I can't *believe* that was nine years ago. Does it seem that long to you?—it seems almost like it was a century ago in another life—and like it was just five minutes ago. It *is* funny how time does that, how its own artificial flavor (its own imagined order we think we want or need) how it just disappears and shifts in the mind when something major happens or is happening between people.

We were *so* young, and yet we were already well into adulthood (in those days where we wondered about our next meals) in that converted hotel-room apartment in Savannah.

I think you were right. I think that period changed everything for me (for *us*) just *everything*. Something about meeting Cole, and then the people I met after that, "the new loves of my life" (as you called them) that now somehow already feel like I've always known them. Something about that changed everything. I never imagined I would be making a living reading books and writing about music and books. I didn't even know that was a job (don't laugh because neither did you. I *remember* your surprise). I guess Cole just saw things I couldn't see yet, and in some ways, I guess *that's* probably the best way I could ever describe her.

O**F COURSE, WE BOTH KNOW I NEVER PLANNED TO BE A PROOFREADER.** I was going to be a songwriter. That was the dream, and I guess, well, I kind of got *near* that, since I do reviews for music and books alongside my proofreading jobs, but that's not quite the same thing. I don't know. I guess I always liked the idea of creating and contributing to written words, but we both *know* I never wanted to be a proofreader, if we even knew what that was back then. Nope, I wanted to be a songwriter. I was going to be a songwriter. I even wrote some songs along the way that you said were just sappy enough to end up on a pop star's record, but I guess life had other plans. I don't know if I ever had much of a plan now that I think about it. I would just listen to (you *remember* this, I *know*, because you still giggle when the song comes on somewhere)—I would just listen to "Visions of Johanna" repeatedly and think, *that's what I want to do.*

I was thinking about this while sitting at a *Starbucks* in Celebration. It is a 24-hour *Starbucks* with a nice, wide, outdoor seating area like Margo always loved. I was sitting outside looking at the neon sign of the **CVS** next door in the middle of the night. I was out roaming around, and I just stopped when I saw the drive-thru was still open. I bought a mocha (you *know* how I love them) and I took a seat on the porch (after parking the car of course) because it was empty, and nobody seems to mind when I do that up in Atlanta. Nobody minded here either. I was sitting on a wooden bench stretching the length of the patio writing in my journal, one of the ones Alex gave me with the cute, pastel covers that remind me of forest air. It was the light green one, the one where I started and failed to keep writing that idea I had for the suspense novel about the domestic abuse survivor in Arkansas named after a city in South Carolina (it was a dumb idea, *or maybe* a great one—I can never tell) and it sits in the first half of that little green notebook like so many other disregarded dreams.

I was avoiding work after sending in my latest essay about music. I'm supposed to proofread this novel about a woman who gets lost in a maze and then finds herself via the help of some kind of magical group of raccoons (or something like that I don't like). I was looking at the half-written (more like tiny scratches of a dream, I guess) Arkansas suspense, and I guess *that's* why I started thinking about how I ended up becoming the one who checks the product of the artists when I originally wanted to *be* the artist. I do realize, as you always said, that each job is probably equally important, and I also know there are many who do both at different times, but it struck me that I would never have expected to make a living this way. It might have been because I was so sure I'd never make much of a living that I only ever considered making art as something to keep me going between factory and fast-food jobs.

It was about three in the morning (I can hear you laughing and asking if I was lonely, but that *was* the time) and I saw this group of people walking across the parking lot. They didn't see me, I don't think. Some were stumbling. Some were normal enough in their walking patterns. I don't know why, but "Visions of Johanna" started playing in my head, and I remembered all those half-thought-out songs I used to write and give up on when I was younger. Maybe it *is* "getting older," as your mom would say, but I sometimes wonder just how many forgotten dreams I left along the way, and I sometimes wonder why I never figured out how to be all that good at follow-through or finishing anything. "I guess those weren't my skills," as Josie would say, if she were here to say anything twenty-plus years after we last spoke. Maybe *that's* why it is always so important to me to finish these letters, maybe our conversations are the one thing I follow through on, or maybe I'm just trying to make everything else make sense.

"DO YOU SELL SEAFOOD?" ASKS THE WOMAN IN THE BLACK SCARF WITH A TATTOO of a dragon on the edge of her arm. The barista looks at her like she might be lost or a little messed up (at two in the afternoon). The barista says what everyone else in the coffee shop is likely thinking, "No, we don't," but leaves unsaid what the rest of us are also likely thinking, *why would you think that?*

The girl in the scarf wants to know if the barista is sure.

The barista looks about as confused as the girl in the scarf now. At the same time, someone with a Midwestern accent exclaims at the sight of, I guess, a loved one, and almost falls out of their chair. At the same time, a young person with darker complexion smiles as they say, "I love you" into the phone they are holding in front of their chest with short, but thick, fingers. As the barista figures out that the girl in the scarf is talking about a sushi place around the corner and begins to end the conversation, a woman in front of me asks if I know any good bars in this neighborhood.

Sometimes I like to watch the people around me as I wait for my coffee (or a chance to *order* my coffee).

I share the above because I know you enjoy my observations. You call them my "zany curiosities," but I like calling them observations. You say it's not pure observation because I have a tendency to invent little stories to go with each person, but I say that detail is not as relevant as you seem to think it is. Right now, I'm sure, you want to know what stories I came up with for the people around me mentioned above, but I didn't bother to do that today. I was too focused on your statement last night. You said we should have dinner together. I'm looking forward to this. You were smiling, but your eyes looked like they did not agree with your lips. You often look like that just before we part ways to go in different directions. It was the same look you had when you went out west and I stayed east. It was the same look you had when you spent years in Texas while I roamed around other states. It was the same look you had when I left for Atlanta, and you said you needed to stay in Athens for a while. I know that look.

It brought me back to the night you showed up in town this time. You said you *missed* me. I said I missed *you*. You said it wasn't "the *same*." I said I didn't understand. You said I *would* understand if I *thought* about it. I've been thinking about it. I've used so many words thinking about it that I may have finally written more than you care to read, "an impossibility," you always say, but maybe this time I did the impossible. I guess I'm thinking about this again because I think you're about to leave again. I don't know for how long this time, but I feel it. I *know* that look. I realize that I may be starting to understand the *differences* in how we miss each other now. I realize that I'm no longer as much of a wreck ("a pile of mess," as Josie would say) when we part ways. It used to almost break my heart each time we were separated, and in some ways—I think I *always* notice on a deep level—even now. At the same time, I guess I'm used to your comings and goings now in ways I wasn't then.

It was *different* back then, and maybe *that's* why I miss you "in a *different* way" now. Everything was *different* back then, I guess, but it's hard to keep that in mind when you and I have always seemed so deeply intertwined. I say *"always,"* but "is anything really *always*?" (you would ask that and I never had an answer).

It *was* different back then. *Then*, I thought you were gone for good each time you left, but *now*, I realize I have other people that matter, so even if you're gone for good I'll find a way, and more importantly, I *now* somehow understand what you said in that forest, off Interstate 10, so long ago. I understand that you're *never* fully gone, that you're *always* with me, even if it's harder to feel it. I think I understand that now. I think I'm starting to understand why you said it was a good thing that I started letting myself connect to other people, though it is still so hard. I guess what I'm saying is I'm ready for our latest "let's-have-dinner," even with that look I know so well in your eyes, and I guess that helps me understand what you said standing by the ball field.

YOU ALWAYS SAID THE CONVERSATIONS WE DIDN'T EXPECT were often the most interesting and important ones we would ever have—*remember* that? I *know* you do, you said it after discussing the pros-and-cons of NGO's for two hours with that lady who never realized you didn't know what an NGO was at the time. Where was that? Were we in St. Louis then? I don't remember. It seems like it was somewhere in the Midwest; it wasn't Chicago or Houston, but like somewhere *deep* in the Midwest where they hold out their vowels and stare a little too long when you speak in a softer voice (or mix and match hair colors on a weekend, like Margo found so interesting to do at the time). Of course, where we were doesn't matter so much in this case, but rather, that I *remember* your conversation, and that you explained why you had it. You said, "you never know, my dear Millie, you never *know* where you might learn something."

I was thinking about this as I watched cars passing me on Fairbanks Avenue the other night. It was later in the evening. It was after our dinner. It was when I already knew you were leaving again. You didn't know for how long this time. You didn't know if we would talk again, the way we always did for so long, until we spent more time alone the last couple years. You told me I should "wrap up the trip." You said I "should figure out *why*" I came to Orlando again. You said I "should go home to Alex." You said I "should talk about all this with Mattie, Tylor, and Cole." You said it was time for my "next chapter." You said it was "time to transmit all these feelings to the *past*, to begin the *future*, feel the *present*."

You said you missed me. I said I missed you too. We both said it wasn't the *same*. We smiled at each other. I told you *I understand*. You said you *knew* I would. You said I needed to "write it all out" for myself, so I could "feel it all." You said it was "important." I believe you. I told you thank you, maybe too many times. You told me there was no need for that. I disagreed. You smiled.

I went out afterward like I always do when we say goodbye until the next time. At first I just walked around the parking lot of the buildings where I'm staying right now. I looked at the walls, the pool I never use, right beside where I park, the lack of people in the nighttime air. I felt the air in my lungs, it was harsher and sweeter than usual, it was like something was making sense inside me that had been hard to grasp at other times. I thought about the 24-hour *Starbucks*, but I wanted something more rustic. I had this memory of you and I talking to those funny artsy people in Tallahassee (what were their names? Abs was one, I think the other was Carina or something like that); it was so long ago, we were so much younger, but we were hanging out at that 24-hour coffee shop that had a name that sounded like a Catholic Church. *All Saints*, that was it, Mattie was there sometime recently and said it's not open 24/7 anymore. I find that sad, but it reminded me of a place called *Austin's on Fairbanks* here in the city.

I was driving to *Austin's* listening to "Strange Currencies" on my car CD player. I was always fascinated with this song when I was a teenager. I found something hopeful in the longing I swore I heard in the vocal delivery. I got to *Austin's*, and there were lovely people here and there, but not *too* many, since it was late at night. I watched a group of teenagers on a couch laughing over an old, beat-up copy of a Madonna album.

You guessed it! It was the one that came with that poster I still carry with me from home to home, though it looks better than it has in years now that Alex framed it to hang in our new place. Alex said it was too important not to be framed properly. I remember you laughed and explained to Alex that I didn't understand the words "framed" and "properly" in the same sentence. It was a nice moment. I was watching the teenagers. I remembered us sitting on similar couches debating whether Janet or Madonna was better (I still say they were equally above all the rest at the time).

I watched another group taking a shared photo on another couch. They looked somewhat androgynous and completely engrossed, and I giggled as the one in the middle snorted (the way Tylor does) at the same time the one on the left shook their head and adjusted their nose ring (with the exact same motion Mattie uses to do the same thing). I felt *that ache*, the one you and Alex call "missing people," I felt it creep up inside me. I walked out on the front porch, and for a moment I just stood there watching the cars. I texted Alex. I told them I was *okay*, and that I missed them. I told them you were leaving. They were not surprised. I think they understood the point of this trip before I did. They often understand me before I do, kind of like *you* do. There were three young women talking at the table just at the edge of the road. They were talking about the difficulties of getting other people to understand bisexualities.

I didn't plan to, but the next thing I knew, I was sitting at the table near them. I was listening to them explain just how hard it was to make others understand attraction that wasn't limited to genitals or gender identities—just like you and I talked about so many times when we "fell in like" (as Josie would put it) with people throughout our travels in the 1990s and 2000s. There was a guy playing banjo (doing *well*, honestly) on the porch at the same time, but I was fascinated by the conversation at the table. It was eerie just how similar the conversation was to the one we had with Josie over 20 years ago at that picnic table that used to sit right in the corner of the park on the main road through Oviedo. I remember we wondered if things would be different for other kids in the future. I sat there realizing that, while many things have changed in the passage of time, this was apparently still a common conversation for kids like us who did not neatly conform to the either/or, pick-a-side ideas of the rest of our nation. Something about this spoke to me, I don't *know* why.

I think it might have had something to do with our goodbye. We both *knew*, we had done this before, we both *knew* you would not show up again in Orlando. I would see you again somewhere else, or I just wouldn't see you again. That was it. You always hated goodbyes, and we didn't really do them well, even in the best of circumstances. You were likely already gone, and that was similar to your comings-and-goings, but it felt *different*. I didn't feel lost. I used to. I expected to be very sad. That was why I thought about going somewhere to watch people, to find myself in unexpected conversations that might seem fascinating. That was not the case. I felt peace, but it was peace with something new. I felt a longing for my life. I wanted to go home, and it felt like I had one. I wondered what Alex was doing in-between text messages. I began thinking about calling this latest adventure finished.

Y OU ASKED HOW THE HELL I CHOSE THIS HOTEL. We were saying goodbye, but randomly, in the middle of all that, you asked what led me to stay at *The Red Lion* of all places. I didn't really have an answer. As you know, Mattie and I like to try random hotels to see what they are like. *Sometimes* this goes very well. There was the time we ended up with a suite bigger than any apartment either of us ever had in Chicago. We had that beautiful view of the greens and the shoreline. It was magnificent. Sometimes this does *not* work out so well. There was that time we ended up in the *Best*

Western in Slidell where the air conditioner held a secret stash of heroin we only found when we were trying to figure out how to work the damn thing. The *Best Western* also had what could only be described as an infestation of every bug known to humans. We didn't stay the night. Instead, we drove to DeRidder and slept in the car across the street from what was once an operational passenger-train line that, by that point, looked like a tourist attraction hidden in a small town no one has ever heard of or bothered to visit. *The Red Lion* decision was another guess.

You were right, I admit, that it was not the kind of nice hotel that I normally like these days.

It's odd to think about what counted as a "good" hotel in the past, and what counts as a "good" one now. I guess the shift in finances and care for my own self has a lot to do with that, but I remember wondering years ago what it would be like to sleep in hotels where I wasn't afraid of something crazy happening in the middle of the night. I must say, it *is* nice. While you were right, this one *isn't* my style, it *is* too-much-tourist for me, but it *is* a nice place. I think it *was* a great decision. I *like* that there are four pools and a volleyball court. Of course, you're laughing now, I can hear it in my head, I don't use these things, but I like seeing them.

I also made *Mattie* giggle when they called the other night because this place has something called fire tables, and neither of us had any clue what the hell *that* was.

It made me think about Alex setting fires outside the pool at that party they took me to with their co-workers. I *know* you remember that party because you thought it was awesome that Alex spent the entire night either beating me up or setting fires—I feel like *that*'s the kind of description that could so easily be used to create a false impression (I now have this image of Alex imitating some action film: beating people up, burning shit down, and cackling like a Gremlin in the moonlight). We both know *that*'s not how it was (but maybe it would make a good short story). I still remember your

133

shock, you were like: "the party had a bouncy house—*what the fuck?*—where do rich folks get these ideas?" and I just laughed. I remember people didn't want to joust with Alex in the bouncy house because Alex kept beating me so easily each time we went in there. Hell, the one time I almost got them, they slipped their weight to the left and tackled me in the middle of the bouncy house. It was fantastic—one of those memories you keep with you forever, like a Polaroid or a Snapshot or something like that, something that belongs in a scrapbook, *that's* what it was like. I think it was *so* wild for people because Alex is, maybe, half my size. I think people thought I would handle them—*you know?* they were like, "Millie has got this, she'll tear Alex up," but they were *so* damn wrong, and I think the shock scared anyone else even *thinking* about entering the bouncy house.

The fire was even more absurd—*remember?* It was colder that night than I'm comfortable with, but the party was mainly outside, and we were drinking beers that were much better cold. There was a bonfire by the pool, or maybe you would call it something else, I don't know. Alex started having fun stoking the fire while I was sitting in one of the long chairs nearby. I was listening as Alex and their co-workers laughed about this-or-that thing, and one of them said Alex should be the fire captain so they could all stay warm—right as Alex was holding a flaming branch over their head, like something out of a superhero movie. I was laughing. Alex was in heaven. The co-workers (with all the usual names) were smiling and cracking jokes. Alex embraced the fire-captain persona, and the rest of the night they were playing with the flames while I watched from beside the pool.

It was another one of those moments that just stuck in my head, and I was sitting there on the phone with Mattie telling them the story again.

Mattie called because they were nervous about visiting some folks they are not too close with in north Florida. They need to do the visit, and they want to know the people much better, but you know how they get nervous about new things. "It's part of who they are," as you say, but it is still hard for them. They were also worried because they had convinced themselves, in a true example of vulnerability gone wild, that they had messed up somehow and made their friend Ella mad at them. They were saying, "she's going to hate me," and I was saying, "it sounds like you didn't do anything wrong, but you're worried you did." I told them to talk to her, and later they did. I was *right*. They were relieved, but it wasn't any easier for them to think they messed up and lost someone special. Don't start with me, I know you don't understand why I can't stand Ella, and that's my business, so don't start, I just don't like her, no big deal. I've told you before, it is almost like she represents every quality I wish I had, that I can't find the courage to cultivate, and that makes me a little insecure when I'm around her. It's no big deal. We get along well enough for the sake of Mattie, that's all that matters.

I guess I don't really know why I picked this hotel. I want to say it was another random pick in the spirit of my and Mattie's adventures. I want to say that *because*, and especially *since*, our last conversation at the house last week, I really miss my people even more than I think I've ever been fully conscious of before now, but I don't know if that's it. *Maybe* I just wanted to be in a tourist part of the city for once after thinking about these areas so much as kids. *Maybe* I just wanted to try something different since it seems like this whole trip is about retracing my steps in an attempt to embrace how different my life has turned out from anything I expected. *Maybe* it's even simpler, and I just liked the thought of getting a really nice, or somewhat nice, place to stay for very little money at the end of this trip. *Maybe* there is no real reason, *and maybe* that's the case with so many decisions that shape a life—but that seems a little too deep to think about, sitting at a fire table in the middle of the night.

PANTING, SWEATING, AND MAYBE EVEN CRYING a little bit, it was the same routine in some ways, though also very *different* than other times I woke from recurring dreams in the past.

I remember you used to listen to me talk about the bad ones. I remember they were *all* bad at one time. I guess *that* is the difference. The recurring dreams were *so* bad when I was just surviving (what did you call it?—when I was *"pretending to be a person,"* all those years before Savannah) the dreams were always nightmares. I wondered if only nightmares could recur. Now, it's a different thing. Sometimes the bad ones come, and when they do Alex or Mattie or Tylor or Ellen will hold me if they're nearby. The good ones, like the bad ones once did, now seem to come all the time. They are, I guess, "like mix tapes in the wind," as Margo said, "pieced together from some of the better moments to put all the ingredients in place."

You had a similar theory about the bad ones, and I think you were right. Mostly, the bad ones, as you know, surrounded the fire in 1998. I lost everything. The house was gone. My family, if you could call them that, was gone. I didn't have anywhere to go. We hit the road to get away from it. It was just after we lost Josie. It was just after those boys assaulted us in the woods and we felt so dirty that we were sure we would never be clean again. It was just after you "took a baseball bat to the throat," as you often put it, "from the asshole with the inferiority complex," as you said it, and you couldn't move your face the same ways you once did when you used to sing. It was all that happening at once, and I know, *I know*, we don't talk about it, but *I* do now, sometimes, with Alex and with my "other loves" that are not like Alex but special in their own ways—and I know, *I know* it was 1998, and that was 20 years ago, but the dreams kept coming, and in the dreams it was never one event, it was all of them and the shit from childhood. It was the beatings. It was the alcohol and drugs. It was the drug dealers with guns in high school. It was the time Josie got assaulted. It was Peter. It was the as-hot-as-possible showers. It was the feeling of being damned, unclean, "cursed," as mother would have said, when she was still breathing in her constant influx of cocktails. It was hell. It was a world out to destroy us.

For so many years, the dreams came. We ran from place to place. We cried and screamed and wished, and died a little bit inside. "The monsters were always right behind us," you said, "we could feel it." I think we both believed that the world *did* destroy us. And it was that way until Savannah. In Savannah it all started to change, and everything stopped making sense for a while. We made sense of it all by somehow convincing ourselves it was all *our* fault. We could have done this *differently*. We could have planned this better. We could have made *this* choice instead of *that* one. We could have come to *that* place instead of *this* one. We could have been faster, slower, more normal, even less normal, more caring and attentive, even less caring and attentive, we could have done *something!*

That was what the dreams were about, I think, it was a mixtape of all the ways we lied to ourselves to convince ourselves we could have stopped it, some of it or all of it, even though we knew on some level it was just a lie we were telling ourselves to try to make what would never make sense somehow make some damn sense. We were trying to control it by making *ourselves* the reason, but what I realized, what the dreams and my brain, I guess, wanted me to see, was that it was never going to make sense because we should never have had to live through any of it in the first place. *None* of it should have happened. *None* of it made sense. *None* of it was our fault. We couldn't have stopped it, but we *wished*, we *tried* to believe we could have stopped it long enough to survive it well enough to someday find good things, things worth living for, again. I think *that's* what the recurring nightmares were about, a reminder that we couldn't stop it, that it wasn't our fault, and that, like the dreams, it was going to happen no matter what we did (or think we could have done) to stop it, we just had to hang on as much as we could.

I think that's also the way the new recurring dreams (the

fantasies, I guess, if I see the old ones as *nightmares*) work. I think it's my mind, myself, I guess, trying to tell me what to hold onto even though I sometimes still think I'm a monster that will mess it all up. I guess that is a side effect of the victim-blaming or the I-could-have-done-something-to-stop-it, survival strategy: I turned myself into the problem, but now I need to keep reminding myself that I am not necessarily a problem and I have others who see that too. I think the new dreams are about *that*. I think it's again my mind trying to keep me aware of something important that is hard for me to see. It puts together a new mixtape of facts, a new transmission, a new broadcast, new truths I need to hear. The dreams show me all the things I love right now, and within this mix, I can see all the ways I love and *am* loved, despite everything I've been through to get here. I can see what it looks like when people are good to each other, when they care. I can see it in my dream, and, maybe somehow, that helps me embrace living, as I continue to try to figure out how in the hell I am ever going to feel like I might be worthy of it.

I think about this as I wake up panting again. I was dreaming I was in a bar that you and I went to in Milledgeville, Georgia. I think the bar is important because none of "my loves" have been to this bar in real life. And I think it's the setting of the mixtape. I think the setting has to be fully about me. But we are watching Mattie's favorite electro-pop band, though they don't tour to Georgia, so I know it's a dream and I'm not sure I would go to an electro-pop show no matter how much I love Mattie, but there they are: Fish Jesus and the Ninja Angels, jamming out in this little hole-in-the-wall bar in Georgia. Then, I notice that the bar is stocked with ciders from Sweden, which would never show up in a bar that doesn't even have a fully functional front door or some mechanism for cleaning the floors. *No, that's* the kind of thing you only find at bars in richer places, but it is also Tylor's favorite drink. This gets even more interesting because there is a corner of the bar that's just a couch, with typewriters like the kind Cole always said she wanted to own, and I don't recall ever seeing such a set up in any bar. Even more hilarious to my eyes, as I roam through the dream, there is a bed in the middle of a messy corner of the bar, where books sit, and Ellen laughs while reading them, kicking the sheets.

Again, find me this bar if it exists.

The real kicker for me is the way that Alex shows up in little hints everywhere. Fish Jesus and the Ninja Angels, for example, are not playing electro-pop tonight, instead they are playing Alice Cooper and Helloween covers, as if Alex picked out the songs for the night. Tylor is wearing a Sisters of Mercy t-shirt and talking to people about a new form of music called Gollum-Core—a mixtape itself of *Lord of the Rings* characters and Heavy Metal that Alex invented with their friend Amara a long, long time ago. The bar is somehow decorated (I mean, this is rural Georgia, remember) in the types of art Alex loves the most, and some of the pieces from our home are prominently displayed. Ellen is explaining the merits of this art (art I have never heard Ellen mention an interest in, of course) to anyone who roams by her reading spot on the bed. Cole is writing research reports about various health issues (like Alex does for a living) instead of her usual fiction, and Mattie keeps writing cute little notes on a white board (like the ones Alex leaves me in our kitchen sometimes when they leave the house). As you once said about my overall life since finding them in Savannah, "Alex is everywhere."

SOMETIMES I STARE AT A CHAIR. I know that sounds odd (well, maybe not to you, but to most people), I bet that would sound odd. *You*, of course, *remember* me staring at couches in store windows because something about the security of liking a home enough to furnish it spoke to dreams hidden inside me. I guess, I still don't know, but that's how you explained it at the time. You probably also remember how funny I thought it was that Mattie's dad went all the way to Chicago to build them a bed that would fit in their tiny apartment. You also probably remember me giggling because I was so deeply in love with Alex's little wooden box. I thought it was amazing that such a small thing, simple wood, could become a permanent fixture full of emotion and meaning. I remember you said you knew you were right, you knew Alex was more than special, you knew it, when I went on and on about a random wooden box.

Anyhow, sometimes I find myself staring at a chair. The chair is at *Austin's,* that coffee shop where you came to see me, the one on Fairbanks Avenue, yeah, that one. Well, it's just a chair, but it is also not just a chair. It reminds me of other chairs, but like some of us in this world, it also stands out due to a simple difference. It is painted as a rainbow, and I know, *I know,* you'll say we all become obsessed with rainbows in our own ways, when we become part of the community, I know, I *know,* but what catches my attention is not the rainbow itself, that's not it. What catches my attention is the distinction, the variance between the rainbow chair and the sea of brown, black, and other more baseline colors throughout the entire building. Everything else is something you would expect to see in a boring furniture catalog, you know (not the *Ikea* catalogue, but a boring one, you know the type). Everything else is like *that,* a sea of beige whispering boring stories about nothing into the floor, and something about that particular forest surrounding this rainbow tree speaks to me, and I think, these almost forty years.

I feel like all the people who followed the rules are hidden in the beige furniture. The ones that only loved who they were told. The ones who swallowed their pain in place and stayed around to pretend it didn't change them. The ones who spoke in whispers or to therapists or to religious leaders only about their truest desires and most uncomfortable fantasies.

The ones who cannot tell you why they have two cars, a house they struggle to afford, or children they only seem to enjoy, at most, occasionally. The ones we make fun of when we eat dinners at *Jason's Deli* because we can't understand how people eating such magnificent food can look so damn unhappy with themselves, the people around them, and maybe even life. I feel like those chairs, the ones that all look the same, the ones that all fit in exactly like they were supposed to, those chairs are the fabrication, but the rainbow one, that one, is real.

It is real in its difference. It is real in its ability to stand out and be an individual thing. It is real in the places where the paint is chipped, the places where this world took a piece and didn't give it back. It is real in the places where there is a notch here or there, the places where it has been, to varying degrees *and maybe* never wholly, repaired from this or that bad moment. It is real in the ways that most people never seem to look at it, they kind of look around it, trying not to see it, trying not to notice that something, anything maybe, could be different with just a little effort, just a bit of risk, just a shot in the dark that might feel terrible, wonderful, or maybe even both. I feel that way when I stare at the chair. I feel real, but also like I'm surrounded by imitations, people who seem fascinated by lives that they would never take the risk to bother trying to live for themselves. I guess that is where I'm heading, I'm becoming someone who no longer feels the need to imitate, someone who simply wants to embrace standing out in the sea of beige, no matter the pain it took to become this way in the first place.

D ESPITE WHAT IT SAYS ON THE SIGN, THE REEDY CREEK STATION IS NOT A STATION, but rather a bus stop on a highway in front of *The Red Lion Hotel*. I don't know why, but I find it fascinating that they have a sign that says it is a **STATION**. It is a bench. It has a garbage can. There is no bag in the can when I look. The directions I got while I was seeking to figure out a way to go somewhere without using my car told me about it. It was sitting in front of my hotel the whole time. I didn't see a station in front of my hotel. I saw a bench that busses stop at. I saw a bench that, while it has a nicer signpost than most, was not, in fact, a station. This got me thinking about the difference between appearance and reality. I know, I know, I've been reading all the Patricia Leavy novels, I know, I'm in love with her brilliance, you can pick on me later, but I have to note that you seemed to know quite a bit about her work for someone picking on me for having a crush, how did that happen?

Anyhow, you have to think about it, the station that is not a station is a perfect example, or at least I think so. The notation of this as a station gives it the impression of a nice, enclosed space where people can go for ease of travel between destinations. However, it is just a bench with a small metal shelter over it that may be useful if the rain doesn't come in sideways. You ever wonder just how evil nature had to be to invent sideways rain? I do. I think about that in relation to us, I guess that's what I'm saying. You are me, but you're not me. I am you, but I'm not you. I don't know how we appear, but we are always connected to each other in some way. I need you, but I also don't need you. You need me, but you probably also don't need me. I miss you and you miss me, but you're right, it's not the same—I get that now. I think I see us more clearly now.

THERE IS A HOTEL ON THE FAR EAST SIDE OF TAMPA. It may be in Brandon, or it may be in Tampa. I'm honestly not sure, and I don't feel like using Google. I am at this hotel. I am standing outside of it. I am watching the people check in for the night. I am not staying here. I will leave Tampa just like I left Orlando about an hour ago. I will go home to Atlanta. I will go home to Alex, to the other loves I have somehow found to share my time with now. I just had to come here, I guess. Especially since it feels like this really is goodbye, at least for a while. I just had to come here one more time before I went to what I now realize is my first real home.

I'm walking to the back of the building. Remember when we came here?— I know you do, but I always ask stuff like that. I know you remember because I know I remember. I guess that's part of this whole post-traumatic-integration thing I've been trying to do by coming back to where you first emerged as something beyond my inner thoughts. I guess that's what you were saying about us missing each other differently. I guess that's why you came by less and less after I met Alex and Mattie and Cole and Ellen and Tylor. I guess that is the point of this long letter, this transmission, like the ones I called journals when I was younger, before 1998, before you came to me in a new way, before we came to this hotel and walked to the back of the building together that night in 1998. It is hard to believe it has been twenty years. It is hard to believe the stairwell is still here. I'm standing beside the entrance to the stairwell. I know you're here. You're inside me like you always were, I can feel you even if I don't need to see you anymore. I'm standing at the wall inside the stairwell. I see it. I see what you wanted us to do. It is still there.

I know you can see it too. I know we have the same eyes. I know we are one. I know that you were right. I know that I needed a friend more than anything, when I had nothing, and no one left to hold onto as I left Orlando, alone. I know you were right. I know that now that I have people to hold onto I don't need you the same way; you will live in my head again, like when I was a kid—I guess when *we* were kids, you would say—you will live there and come back out if I ever need you again; thank you for that. I know I'm thanking myself, my survival instinct, you would say, but thank you all the same. I stare at what you had me write on the wall. The graffiti around it has grown over the years, from the minds of other travelers on missions of their own. All of it seems alike except for what I wrote. What I wrote feels sacred. I can see it. It still says the same thing. I can hear it. I stand here where we started, and I know I need to read it aloud to myself:

My name is Millie Morrison. They named me something else, but they were WRONG. They COULD NOT BREAK me, NOTHING could. I WILL SURVIVE.   MY NAME IS MILLIE MORRISON.

I CHOOSE TO LIVE.

I WILL SURVIVE.

I WILL START

A NEW CHAPTER, A BETTER LIFE, SOMEDAY—

JUST WAIT AND SEE.